AUTHOR	CLASS
JOCKS, Y.	F

TITLE   Say goodnight, Gracie

be visiting

SAY GOODNIGHT, GRACIE

Yvonne Jocks

ZEBRA BOOKS
Kensington Publishing Corp.
http://kensingtonbooks.com

ZEBRA BOOKS are published by

Kensington Publishing Corp.
850 Third Avenue
New York, NY 10022

All Kensington titles, imprints and distributed lines are available at special quantity discounts for bulk purchases for sales promotion, premiums, fund-raising, educational or institutional use.

Special book excerpts or customized printings can also be created to fit specific needs. For details, write or phone the office of the Kensington Special Sales Manager: Kensington Publishing Corp., 850 Third Avenue, New York, NY 10022. Attn. Special Sales Department. Phone: 1-800-221-2647.

Zebra and the Z logo Reg. U.S. Pat. & TM Off.

First Printing: January 2004
10 9 8 7 6 5 4 3 2 1

Printed in the United States of America

Sisters. Weddings.
To Meg and Duane.

Chapter One

It's not so very different from climbing a mountain, Grace Sullivan cheered herself, carefully finding one runner-carpeted step, then the next, without looking. *Except for the book on my head.*

She couldn't see her feet, in their neatly buttoned kid-leather boots, because of that book—her mother's well-worn copy of *A Lady's Guide to Society and Deportment.* She couldn't even see the red carpet runner, except for six steps ahead of her, or any other glimpses of the Sullivans' fine Colorado Springs home.

And I don't generally stumble or break things in the mountains, she reminded herself, closing her eyes and pretending. *So if I only imagine that this—*

Suddenly, the banister hit her in the tummy. She abruptly stopped, eyes flying open. The book, not so encumbered, kept going.

And it was such a large, heavy book.

SMASH!

Grace peeked tentatively over the edge of the banister, wincing even before she saw that *A Lady's Guide to Society and Deportment* had landed in the midst of her mother's collection of porcelain pastoral figurines, which crowded the sideboard beside the stairway.

"Oh, dear. . . ." she whispered.

This was not a mountain. She'd probably only survived the mountains, or the mountains survived her, because she'd been a child instead of a woman of almost eighteen. Besides, unlike Mama's crowded showplace of a home, the mountains hadn't been quite so . . . fragile.

If they had been, Grace Sullivan surely would have broken them.

At least it was her oldest sister, Belle, whose head poked out of the adjoining parlor to survey this most recent disaster. She rolled her eyes up at Grace with affectionate exasperation as she swept to the sideboard to fix what she could. And Belle did sweep. Even back when she'd thought herself plain, she'd been graceful.

Belle wasn't plain now. In just the past year she'd become very, very pretty. Her once-rusty hair now glowed almost auburn, and her freckles were hardly visible since she'd started using a parasol, and she wore the most stylish clothes and carried the prettiest fans Grace had seen in all her years.

Unlike many, Grace had *always* thought her tall, vibrant eldest sister pretty. If Belle had found true beauty, it likely wasn't so much the dresses or the hair rinse as the simple fact that Belle was engaged to be married.

Love added a glow to the older girl's cheeks and a spring to her step that no wardrobe or new coiffure could ever have provided. Grace felt quite certain of that. After all, she'd seen a similar glow ignite in their middle sister, Charisma, whose engagement was more recent.

And she'd seen how worn their mother looked of late, the longer she fought with Da.

Remembering the discord that haunted the Sullivan household, Grace—already on her way down the stairs to help—decided to hurry, lest Mama see this latest damage and become even more upset. On the third-to-the-last step she caught the hem of her skirt under one foot and began to fall, but caught herself against the newel post and swung full around on it in a way that would have been fun . . . if it weren't so hoydenish.

Of the many things she'd broken since the family moved to this fine house in Colorado Springs almost seven years ago, Grace never seemed to break herself.

"Do have a care, dearest," cautioned Belle as she swept shards of porcelain—a shepherdess's crook, a glazed sweep of ceramic pinafore—from the sideboard and into her palm, then into her dress pocket. "Our parents are feeling particularly sour today."

"We knew it couldn't last," agreed a second voice. Their middle sister, Charisma, floated down the stairs as she came to join them in the foyer. Why did only Grace's feet make pounding noises, when Grace was the smallest? Charisma, with her strawberry blond hair and blue-green eyes, had always been both pretty *and* graceful. All Charisma ever wanted had been tact.

Like now. Even now, Grace felt a stab of panic at her middle sister's words. "What couldn't last?"

Mama and Da?

"How happy everyone was after Will announced our engagement." Charisma cocked her head at Grace's visible upset. She had not meant anything upsetting—after all, she *had* improved in charm lately. "We keep thinking that if we can only put Mama at ease about our prospects, she might stop fighting with Papa, but I'm beginning to wonder if it is of any use at all."

But . . . it just *had* to help the problems between their parents! Belle would be marrying the son of a British viscount, and Charisma was engaged to a fine lawyer who had very nearly won the recent senatorial race. Their mother's fervent wish for them to escape their past as the children of a struggling miner, living in a company shanty, seemed to have been granted.

Really, truly granted, considering the wishes . . .

But Belle and Charisma were not the only Sullivan girls who had wished themselves a better future the previous spring, out among the twisting red rock formations in the nearby Garden of the Gods. The particular stone the sisters had wished at was the Three Graces, a triple spire said to represent the idealized images of Beauty, Charm, and Grace. Since beauty, charm, and grace were exactly what the Sullivan sisters needed, their wishes had made sense. Better yet, over the past year they seemed to be coming true!

Just like magic, Grace thought, and as ever, the thought pleased her.

Belle had found both inner and outer beauty with the help of the Honorable Christopher Stanhope.

Charisma had found direction, and a far sweeter

nature, on the arm of William Barclay, a senator's aide.

But, Grace . . .

"It's because I still don't have a beau," she admitted, reaching among the collection of sleek figurines to help Belle with the cleanup. "Once I win someone Mama approves of—"

"Of whom Mama approves," corrected Charisma smoothly.

". . . then perhaps she'll truly believe that Da hasn't ruined our chances at happiness, and they can love each other again. I just need to become more graceful, the way you—"

But even as Grace spoke, her anxious hand accidentally nudged over another figurine. Its arm snapped off on impact.

Grace bit her lip and tried not to let her upset crawl out of her throat. This was her fault. Her sisters did not have this problem. And yet . . .

She tried so *hard*!

"Here, dearest." Charisma carefully guided Grace's hand out of the pastoral display of now-wounded porcelain figures and handed her the book to hold. "Let me do that."

As Belle finished clearing the fragments and dust left by the book's initial impact, Charisma scooted several of the figurines around so that there were no empty spots in their arrangement. After a moment's consideration, she turned the wounded goose girl away, so her missing arm didn't show, and tucked that extra arm into a ceramic milkmaid's pail. "There. Mama rarely pays attention to all the knickknacks she buys; she should never even notice. We simply need to speak to the housekeeper and ask her not to point it out herself. Why don't I do that?"

Charisma truly had become increasingly adept at negotiation. As a politician's wife, she would have to be.

"*Your* wishes were granted," Grace reminded her sisters in a low voice. Nobody but the three of them knew what they'd truly wished on that fateful picnic, after all. Well, them and the Three Graces. "Belle got prettier and won Mr. Stanhope. And Charisma learned to be more charming and caught Mr. Barclay. If I can just learn to be more graceful, then perhaps I'll find a man Mama approves of just as much."

"Of whom Mother approves," corrected Charisma—but she seemed to be sharing a secret glance with Belle.

"And then she can be happy," Grace finished, but with increasing suspicion. "What is it?"

Belle hesitated, but Charisma confessed, "We think your help may be en route."

"It was meant to be a surprise," added Belle.

Charisma said, "Mama has sent for a teacher, all the way from Paris! She should be here by month's end."

Grace blinked at them. She knew she should celebrate receiving help at last, but instead, she felt oddly like an old boot dropped off at the cobbler's without its consent. That was silly. Of course she wanted help. Except . . .

"It's not just for the clumsiness," Belle assured her.

"Oh, no," Charisma added. "Comtesse Arabella is a *connoisseur of feminine comportment*."

"Kit doesn't know her," admitted Belle. "But he says there are a great many noblewomen he doesn't know, despite the rumors."

Kit was Belle's fiancé, and Grace liked him. He was certainly proof that coming from a noble background wasn't necessarily a bad thing.

"Comtesse Arabella," Grace repeated carefully, and it did sound like a terribly graceful name. "Do you think she can truly help? Even me?"

"It has not escaped us," explained Belle, lowering her voice, "that neither Charisma nor I managed our transformations alone. I had the help of Miss Keithley, and of the dressmaker, Madame Aglaia."

"And I received assistance from the widow Pappadopoulos," added Charisma. "So if our wishes really are being granted, why would you not receive help, too?"

"Comtesse Arabella," repeated Grace, more hopefully. "She may make me elegant yet!"

"If that's what you really want," said Charisma. But of course it was what Grace wanted. To embarrass her family no longer. To win a socially acceptable husband so that Mama would stop worrying. To—

A door slammed open from the dining room, full proof that the task of easing Mama's worries would be a challenging one.

"Bringing all manner of rough men into our home!" Mama exclaimed, sailing ahead of their new cook in the direction of her husband's office. "Does he not have a care for his own daughters or their fragile reputations?"

Belle and Charisma exchanged another secret look at that. Then Belle, in several long strides, intercepted their mother's latest complaint. "Mama? Whatever's the matter?"

"Your father is the matter!"

Charisma whispered, "As if we expected anything else."

Grace bit her lip and stayed silent.

"He has the audacity to invite ne'er-do-wells to waltz right in off the street, as if they belong here! What would either of your good affianced husbands think, should they come to visit and find ruffians amongst us? What might become of poor Grace's reputation?"

Actually, ruffians sounded interesting. Grace stopped worrying her lip so hard and glanced again at Charisma.

"*Ruffians,* Mama?" asked Grace's middle sister. "In Colorado Springs?"

"Begging your pardon, ma'am," murmured their latest cook. The dark-haired, matronly woman had come all the way from one of Denver's elite restaurants to work for them. She had a long and foreign-sounding name, so everyone except Charisma—who felt strongly about things like equality—called her Cook. "He did come to the back door instead of the front."

For all her faults, Mama—who'd once had to work as a domestic herself—rarely condescended to the servants. She simply answered, "He ought not be coming to this house at all, and even Mr. Sullivan should know that much!" Then she continued her march toward the den. "MISTER SULLIVAN!"

Grace saw both Belle and Charisma wince. She suspected that their fiancés, were they here, would be as taken aback by Mama's bellow as they would by the presence of ruffians. Not that they would hold either Mama or ruffians against the women they loved—they'd already proved that much.

Grace loved watching how in love her sisters were. But her parents . . .

"MISSSSTERRRRR SULLLLL—"

The door from Da's den slammed open, and the battle royal began. "Bridey Sullivan, you can call me Paddy like you always used to do, or Patrick if you're of a mood, but otherwise you can keep your tongue in your head! This is my home. I'll not be referred to as if by one of my employees!"

Which, sadly, was just the opening Mama needed. "If this is indeed your home, sir, then why would you invite some common gold miner to bring his business here? Surely the mining offices are a far more appropriate place than this quiet haven, which I have struggled so valiantly to provide for your innocent daughters."

Da strode around the foot of the staircase to the foyer, clearly looking for somebody. "Erikson's here?"

"I asked him to wait in the kitchen." Mama put her hands on her hips in full challenge.

Even when Da slowly turned back to her, full Irish rage in his face, Mama hardly flinched. She only flinched—briefly—when Da roared, *"YOU . . . DID . . . WHAT?"*

Then she launched her own counterattack, and even the promise of ruffians couldn't protect Grace from that sick, dizzy feeling she got when they yelled like this. Her parents had magnificent voices, shaking the chandeliers, bouncing off Mama's hundreds of knickknacks, echoing from the shelves and paintings and dark-paneled walls.

Cook backed carefully away toward the kitchen.

"Come along, Grace," murmured Belle, herding her sisters up the stairs. "We should give them privacy."

"And hope that Kit and Will don't show up until the storm passes," muttered Charisma.

Clutching her book tightly to her stomach, like she might a favorite doll, Grace followed miserably up the stairs, only occasionally stepping on her sisters' skirts—they were adept at sweeping hems neatly out of her path. If becoming graceful and winning an advantageous beau would help keep Mama from blaming Da for everything, then she longed to do just that. She had to! It was her duty.

But she had to wonder why Cook, lingering in the doorway by the dining room, smiled slowly up at her as if in silent encouragement.

When Jon Erikson first saw the house—a tall brick mansion, really—he wondered if he should even have come. He was looking for one of his father's old friends from the men's younger days back East, not for a millionaire silver king! That was why he'd gone around to the back door, for fear that he'd gotten the wrong house.

But the cook assured him that this was indeed Mr. Patrick Sullivan's home, and sent for Mrs. Sullivan. That's when the trouble started. Mrs. Sullivan was dressed to the nines—was that normal for the middle of the day, even in a mansion? Jon reckoned so. From the way she looked him over, his own clothes— good, sturdy jeans, work boots, suspenders, and a chambray shirt—clearly were *not*.

It unsettled him, her displeasure. Normally, women of all ages took an immediate shine to him.

"Mr. Sullivan left word at his office for me to come here," he explained carefully, trying not to let any trace of his parents' immigrant lilt color his words. He was dark blond for a Norwegian—his hair closer to honey than to buttermilk—but she would hear his background in his name. An accent on top of it would likely seem as ugly to a society lady like this as if he'd tracked in mud on his boots. "I didn't mean to intrude."

"How could he?" demanded Mrs. Sullivan, startling Jon with her full Irish brogue. Then she simply turned and stalked away, as if hunting something. He pitied that something. Mrs. Sullivan's voice echoed back at them. *"MISTER SULLIVAN!"*

The cook placed a mug of coffee and a plate with several pastries on the kitchen table, an apologetic look on her face. "Please, Mr. Erikson, have some refreshments while we fetch the master."

So he sank into the indicated chair, which felt too small for him, and he listened to the fight echoing back at him from the front of the mansion. It was raw enough to have garnered wagers, if he could have guessed a winner—and if anybody were around to cover him.

And Jon ate. He wasn't such a fool as to turn down good food. One sip of the richest coffee ever to caress his tongue, and one taste of the gooey, flaky nuts-and-honey-strewn pastry made him glad for that policy.

After all, he had no reason to concern himself with the Sullivans' lives. One of the things he most loved about prospecting was that it kept him from the snare of trying to impress fancy society types like Mrs. Sullivan.

Or, considering her own volume and accent, like Mrs. Sullivan *pretended* to be.

The lady's complaint, from what Jon could hear, was that Mr. Sullivan ought to conduct his business at the mine office. He certainly should not invite riffraff—like Jon, apparently—into the delicate confines of her home. It seemed they had daughters to worry about. Apparently, those daughters had beaux who would prefer not to rub elbows with a common laborer.

It was enough to make Jon consider shouldering his pack and heading out. He wouldn't stop until he found a camp somewhere in the mountains above Colorado Springs, away from such petty worries. But he'd promised his father, and Jon kept his promises.

Besides, the mountains were right cold this time of year. No reason to head out on an empty stomach.

Mr. Sullivan's position was that he'd bought the blasted house and thus could invite anyone he chose, and that their daughters had the sense to differentiate between good men and bad by better proof than their clothing, praise God—and speaking of God, which one of His angels or the saints gave Mrs. Sullivan the right to mistreat his invited guests?

That sent them into a fracas about Mr. Sullivan's behavior at her parties, and why people rarely attended.

Jon sighed, chanced distracting God with quick thanks that he was unmarried, and took another bite of pastry.

Then he noticed a little boy staring at him from behind a cracked doorway. Cute kid. Black hair in long, loopy curls. Large black eyes with thick, black lashes. Button nose with freckles. Maybe seven years old.

Before Jon could even offer the child a pastry, the boy noticed his attention. His eyes, against all probability, got even wider—

Then he was gone. The door, either to a pantry or a cellar, stood cracked but empty.

Huh.

In the meantime, the Battle of the Sullivans had turned. Mrs. Sullivan screamed that her husband cared nothing for his girls or their future. Mr. Sullivan asked God never to let him care so selfishly that it meant scorning good working-class men— and he asked it loudly enough, Jon suspected that God Himself might hear the request personally. One door slammed. Another door slammed. Something broke.

Silence descended over the house while Jon sipped more coffee. Then, a moment later, the door to the kitchen opened, and the cook reappeared. "Mr. Sullivan will see you now," she announced as he rose.

He nodded and started to follow her out, checking to make sure he *hadn't* tracked in mud. On second thought, he veered back to the table to grab the second pastry and stuffed it in his mouth as he passed.

He never ate this well in the gold fields.

By the time they reached the hallway outside Patrick Sullivan's office, Jon had not only swallowed the treat, but wiped his big hands carefully on his jeans. He might be riffraff, but at least when he shook hands with his father's old friend, who emerged from the office to greet him, he wouldn't be sticky. "Hello, sir," he greeted. "I'm—"

"Erikson!" exclaimed Patrick, surprising him with a quick, hard hug. "Even if I weren't expecting you, it's recognizing you I'd be; you're the image of your da, sure enough."

Maybe in appearance. But Jon's father had made mistakes that Jon himself meant to avoid. "Thank you. Pa remembered you fondly, too." He swallowed back the catch that sometimes hurt his throat when he thought of the letter he still carried, informing him of his father's death. "When I told him I was Colorado-bound, he made me promise to find you and—"

But the strangest thing interrupted him. It was a book. A large book. And it plummeted down onto the carpeted stairway and then bounced beside the two men, as if from the sky. It bounced.

"Oh!" exclaimed a female voice from the same direction.

Jon and Mr. Sullivan looked at each other and then, as one, leaned over the banister to look up the stairs. Past the first landing. Past the second. All the way up to the top floor.

Uff da, he thought—Norwegian for *uhoh*.

A red-haired girl was hanging precariously by one arm, all petticoats and blue skirt and white-stockinged legs, easily twenty feet above them. "Oh, dear!" she moaned.

Then her hand slipped, and with a cry she plummeted after her book.

Chapter Two

But I never *hurt myself,* Grace thought, foolishly confused as her fingers lost their grip on the edge of the landing.

Falling frightened her anyway. So did the yells—her own scream, Belle's from the second-floor landing, Da's cry of *"GRACE!"* beneath her. She barely had time to screw her eyes shut, hoping she would not die . . .

And then, with a soft thud, she was tight in someone's arms—and she landed. It didn't hurt at all! In fact, she felt warm and safe, and her landing cushion smelled wonderfully of fresh air and mountains. Grace opened her eyes and found herself nose to nose with the handsomest man she'd ever, ever seen.

He lay beneath her on the bottom steps, where he'd clearly vaulted the banister and caught her. *Rescued* her!

He had an honest, sun-browned face and sun-streaked golden hair, and eyes as pale a blue as the Colorado sky in summertime—eyes gazing back up into hers. Drawing her head back slightly, she noticed his lips, too. She'd never thought a man's lips could look so very soft.

"Grace!" cried Da again, falling to his knees beside the tangle of his youngest daughter and this strong, brave man, catching her face between grateful hands. "Oh, my darlin', you gave me such a fright!"

Then Mama's screech gave everyone a fright. "Grace Sullivan! Your *stockings*! Your *BLOOMERS*!"

Grace barely had a chance to blush at how her fall must have disheveled her dress, before Mama had swept down upon her, one hand tugging her daughter's clothing back into place, and her other . . .

Oh, dear! Mama was hitting Grace's hero!

"How dare you?" exclaimed Mama, doing her best to beat the blond man away from Grace with all the ferocity of a mother bear—and an Irish one—despite that Grace was on top of him. "How *DARE* you come into my house and molest my children!"

"Bridey!" exclaimed Da—but at least he was laughing this time, partly from relief, partly from sheer admiration. He caught Mama around the waist to draw her back while Grace rolled self-consciously off her savior to smooth her own skirts down farther. Her blush felt hotter.

She shyly caught the gaze of the man who'd saved her, and he tried to smile at her. His teeth were strong and white, which did not surprise her at all, but despite his dimples, it looked more like a wince. Surely Mama hadn't hurt him. A strapping man like that?

And yet when Mama clawed her way out of Da's restraining hold and fell on the stranger again, hitting with both hands, the blond man did indeed wince—and tried awkwardly to crab backward, up the stairs and away from Mama's fury.

"Bridey, it's not what you think," insisted Da, catching her back again while Belle and Charisma ran down the stairs to join the excitement. Their feet made noise this time. "She fell, darlin'. She fell, is all, and young Erikson caught her, bless his soul! Else our Grace might've been . . ." Perhaps he didn't want to imagine what she might have been.

Mama gaped. "She . . . fell?"

In the meantime, Belle caught Grace into a hug so tight, Grace could hardly breathe. Though that could partially be from the fall, too.

Or from "young Erikson's" summertime blue eyes.

"Yes, ma'am," gasped Grace, past Belle's shoulder. "From all the way on the third floor. But he caught me." As soon as she could twist from Belle's grasp, then Charisma's, Grace turned with a true smile to where her rescuer still sprawled beside her book, all long legs and broad shoulders and crooked arms, on the carpeted steps. But he couldn't see her smile, because his eyes were closed. Even when he opened them, he seemed somehow less inclined to return the pleasantry than before.

In fact, he seemed oddly pale beneath his sun-darkened skin.

"Thank you," said Grace. "You may have saved my life."

The blond man attempted a smile. It was a terrible attempt. "You're welcome," he sort of gasped.

Which was when quick Charisma finally noticed what the others, in their concern over Grace, had not seen.

"Oh, my God!" she exclaimed. "Look at his leg."

* * *

It was broken, all right.

The Sullivans sent for the doctor and waited anxiously for his diagnosis, but Jon had known his right leg was broken since the moment Grace Sullivan landed on him. He'd both heard and felt the bone snap.

The wonder that was Patrick Sullivan's youngest daughter was such a pleasure, Jon had barely noticed the pain for several long, amazing moments of heaven, lying beneath her. She'd felt soft, and curvy, and petite—not that even small missiles couldn't do damage, from enough height—and she had bright red hair that trailed softly across his neck, wide gray-blue eyes, and an upturned nose. He thought she had to be the prettiest girl he'd ever seen, and he'd seen some pretty ones. When he'd realized that his fingers were touching her stockinged leg where her skirt had fallen high, he'd felt certain of it.

Then her mother had attacked, and feeling had returned to other areas of his body, and he'd remembered his broken leg. That was when it had really started to hurt. Despite several medicinal swallows of Mr. Sullivan's fine whiskey, Jon's leg didn't hurt any less once the doctor finished setting it in the family's fine parlor. And it was not as if the parlor, with archways opening into both the foyer and the dining room, afforded him much privacy.

He'd done well not to cry out. But he doubted he'd managed stoicism, whiskey or not.

"I'm sorry," Grace repeated, wringing her hands. "Oh, Mr. Erikson, I'm so very sorry!"

"Pshaw," he dismissed, trying to wave the apology aside. His wave felt only a little unsteady—whether from the whiskey or the pain, or the memory of how curvy and soft the lady's leg had felt, he wasn't sure. "I can hardly feel it. And better me than you."

He meant that, too—the last part. She was too pretty to be hurt. Even when she fell from . . . from . . .

He squinted at her, curious. And anxious to keep her talking to him. "How *did* you manage to fall like that?"

Grace covered her mouth with both hands and squeaked out a noise that sounded vaguely like a wounded dog. She looked like she was going to cry.

"No!" he protested. "I didn't mean to upset you." He turned in desperation to the older girls, who were seated in a neat semicircle around him. "I didn't mean to upset her."

"That's all right, Mr. Erikson," said Belle, patting his hand. "Grace is just sorry that she hurt you, is all."

Grace, still covering the lower half of her face, nodded fervently.

"Pshaw," said Jon again, with another wave. "It wasn't her fault. I've had worse."

Though never when he was quite this short on funds. And never this far from his former home in Minnesota. When the doctor left with Mr. Sullivan, Jon guessed Sullivan had just extended him credit. He didn't like that. Debt was a bad deal, no matter the circumstances.

But he was sure enough too broke to fight even a bad deal. And worrying about where he'd stay to heal up, what with having no job, and winter piling up the snow outside, took precedence even over paying the doctor.

That's when a shout from the foyer archway, from the lord of the manor, caught not only his attention but that of the three ladies sitting with him.

"A *boarding house*?" exclaimed Patrick Sullivan again. "No, Bridget Sullivan, I'll not be sending the man to a boarding house, nor a hospital, either. He saved our daughter's life. He will remain as our guest until that leg of his is fit enough for him not just to walk, but to dance a jig!"

Which could solve Jon's immediate problems, except—

"Mr. Sullivan," insisted his wife, her voice trembling with her effort to keep it even—despite a clear flush of upset across her cheeks, "I beg you to consider your daughters' reputations."

"Me name's Patrick!" bellowed Sullivan. "Unless you're working for me, I'd thank ye to call me such! And any reputation that requires our girls to put a wounded man out on the streets is no reputation they need to be courting!"

"But their fiancés!"

"Belle and Charisma chose men with good heads on their shoulders," insisted Sullivan. "Stanhope and Barclay will see reason."

Their argument continued in that vein. Jon's attention moved uncertainly back to the sisters. *Fiancés?* The idea left him troubled—as if the availability of any society debutantes meant a wooden nickel to a dirt miner like himself.

The oldest one, Belle, nervously twisted an engagement ring around her finger as she looked down at the fine carpet. Her blush showed bright freckles Jon hadn't noticed before, what with his being in intense pain and all. And distracted.

Charisma stared at her parents with her chin high, a mixture of dismay and annoyance on her handsome face. Jon saw that she, too, wore a single blue sapphire on her ring finger.

And Grace . . .

She'd lowered her hands to her lap—and they were free of rings.

Jon's relief was likely as foolish as his upset had been. Grace Sullivan was from the world of tall brick mansions, servants, kitchen entrances, and . . . and parlor knickknacks. More knickknacks than he'd ever seen in his life. Jon's world was sleeping outside, the stars bright above him, the smell of dirt deep in his lungs, the feel of cold water and stone on his hungry hands.

Free or not, Grace Sullivan surely would not have him, even if he wanted her. And he knew better than to ever want someone like her.

And yet, watching the misery deepen in her wide eyes as her parents' argument dragged on, Jon wanted *something*. He wanted to make the hurt stop.

And not the hurt in his leg. The hurt in Grace Sullivan.

"Because I am your husband!" exclaimed her father, and the room fell hushed as everyone stared at his wife.

It was a dangerous line for the man to draw.

Without another word, though clearly she was swallowing a gulletful back, Bridey Sullivan spun and stalked from the parlor, her bustle swinging furiously behind her.

The whole room seemed to sigh in guarded relief. Grace's wide eyes and pressed lips still showed more fear than anything.

"You'll be staying in our third-floor guest room," announced Sullivan, as heartily as if he'd not just naysayed his own wife in front of them all to wrangle the invitation. "And you'll let me pay your doctor bills. I insist. 'Tis about time this blasted money went to something worthwhile for once."

But his insistence wasn't what swayed Jon. Normally, Jon wouldn't have stayed where his welcome was questionable, crippled leg or not. Not for all the gold in the Rockies. Especially not in a fancy, overcrowded residence like this one, with its vases of tall feathers and its picture-and-mirror-covered walls and its silver and its statues and its carpets.

But for the chance to see a little more of pretty Grace Sullivan, and perhaps to ease a little of the upset in her blue eyes, he reckoned he could put up with a lot worse than a chance to recover.

"I'll pay my own doctor bills," he countered all the same. "As soon as I can afford it."

Patrick Sullivan came to his side—carefully stepping around the ottoman where Jon's splinted leg was extended—and took his hand to seal the bargain. "But only once you can afford it easily," the older man insisted.

Jon figured they could argue that point later. Sometime when he didn't feel so dizzy. Or in pain. Or so very glad to have a pretty redheaded girl smile at him the way Grace Sullivan suddenly smiled at him.

Besides, at that point he noticed a curly black head peeking around the archway into the dining room—the same little boy he'd seen before. Jon noticed wide dark eyes taking in his injury, so he winked deliberately to put the child at ease.

Then two very well-dressed men in tailored suit coats entered the parlor from the foyer—one pale blond and sharp-featured, the other darker and more solemn. From the way Belle and Charisma Sullivan leaped up to greet them, these were the fiancés he'd been hearing about.

They were from the world of mansions and carpets, too. He could tell, just to look at their clothes.

Since Grace still sat beside him, Jon tried to catch her attention with an uneven grasp of her wrist and whispered, "Who's that little boy I keep seeing?"

But maybe it came out louder than he'd intended, because everyone looked confused.

The blond man—Belle's—asked in a crisp British accent, "Dearest, why are you entertaining a drunken prospector with a broken leg? Not that I mean criticism," he added quickly when Mr. Sullivan's eyes narrowed dangerously. "To the family or the invalid. I assure you, I am merely curious."

Grace said, in answer to Jon's question, "What little boy?"

And Jon wondered, ashamed, if he really was drunk.

"He's *wonderful,*" decided Grace. She liked how that sounded, saying it out loud, even if it was just to Cook. "And Kit and Will—I mean, Mr. Stanhope and Mr. Barclay—they seemed to like him too, while they were helping Da carry him up the stairs to the guest room. Especially after Charisma told them how Mr. Erikson saved my life."

Jon Erikson. It was a *wonderful* name.

She leaned on the table in the middle of the kitchen and watched Cook ladle soup into a small tureen from the kettle on their large cast-iron stove. The stove gleamed black and silver, as clean and sleek as everything in this fine kitchen in their fine house. She had vague memories of Da insisting that Mama have the best kitchen money could buy, because of how fine her cooking was.

That was back when Mama had still cooked for them, back when her parents still seemed to love each other.

Still, Grace loved being in the kitchen—the heat, and the scent of apples and onions and cheese, and the very *cleanness* of it. Kitchens got messy so quickly; bits of them were always being scrubbed. It made the kitchen feel . . . brighter than other rooms.

This new cook, dark-haired and stout, was the first in ages to allow Grace to spend time here. As long as Grace kept very still and didn't touch anything, of course. She even sometimes talked with Grace. Like now.

"What is there not to like?" Cook asked.

"Exactly," agreed Grace. But a niggling piece of discontent rubbed at her, like a pebble in her shoe—and she knew it would only get worse if she did not admit it. "Except for him being a miner."

"Isn't your father a miner?" Cook snipped bits of cilantro off one of the pots of herbs that she'd brought with her when she came from Denver, then sprinkled those snips into the tureen.

Grace laughed. She hadn't heard her father called a miner for years. "He owns mines, anyhow," she said. "And you're right—he used to prospect. That's not the problem. It's just that . . . Mr. Erikson is a laborer."

Cook paused in tying the lid onto the tureen with a napkin to stare expectantly at Grace.

"Not that there's anything wrong with laborers as a class," Grace added quickly. In fact, when she thought back to her youth in Leadville and remembered Da trudging home dirty and sweated through from his work, and how happy her family had been . . . she wondered why advancing socially had required leaving that behind. "But Mama would never allow me to associate with one. Ladies ought not have male companions, outside their relatives, of course, except as family friends and prospective suitors. Mr. Erikson . . ."

She remembered what he'd felt like on the stairs, his long body so solid and warm under her own. She remembered noticing his lips. She wondered what it would be like to kiss such lips as those.

She felt strangely dizzy, but in a surprisingly nice way—until she remembered the point she'd been making.

"Mama wants me to marry well," she explained. "Like Belle and Charisma. She wants me to be courted by bankers, or cattle barons, or railroad tycoons. Or a silver king, like Da."

Even if Da hated being called a silver king.

"But younger," she added, while Cook opened the oven door, releasing a cloud of bread-scented warmth. Heaven!

"What do *you* want?" asked Cook, retrieving a pan of golden biscuits.

Me? Grace was almost as surprised by the question as she was by the sudden thought of blue eyes, eyes as blue as a Colorado sky in summertime. But she tried always to be honest, so she thought about her answer a moment, then said, "I want my parents to be happy again."

"No matter the cost?" challenged Cook.

How much had her parents already given up for her future? Da no longer pretended to disguise his dislike of this showplace of a house, one of Mama's greatest prides. Mama had struggled against an elitist society for years, enduring ridicule and embarrassment so that her daughters would not have to suffer the hardships she once had. They'd both sacrificed more than Grace could probably imagine.

How could she not willingly sacrifice in return?

"Mr. Erikson never gave indication that he wished to be a suitor, anyway," she reminded Cook. "He was here to see Da, not me."

And now she'd gone and broken the man's leg! Better—and safer for him—that she simply stay out of his way while he mended.

"There," Cook said, draping a blue-checked napkin over the basket in which she'd settled the covered soup pot and hot biscuits. Then she looked up at Grace through her lashes. "Miss Grace, I wouldn't normally ask this, but my knees get so stiff in this weather. Would you be willing to deliver this to Mr. Erikson for me?"

And despite everything she'd just said about miners and laborers and sacrifice, Grace wanted nothing so much as to see Mr. Erikson again. She shouldn't deliberately *avoid* him, should she? And Grace had apologized a great deal, but had she thanked him yet?

She thought she might have, on the stairs. But her memory of what had happened, lying on top of him, was a little muddled.

And yet something else made her hesitate. "I'll spill it," she whispered, suddenly terrified.

"Don't jinx yourself so," scolded Cook. But she'd only been working here for a few weeks. She did not know how clumsy Grace could be. "We will use the dumbwaiter, so you needn't carry the soup on the stairs."

Grace shook her head. "I'll spill it on him."

"Put it on the bed table, then step back and let him do the rest." Cook made it sound so temptingly simple. "He seemed to be a particularly capable young man even with a broken leg, didn't you think?"

Oh, yes. Very capable. So capable that he'd managed to break her fall. So capable that he hadn't shouted once while the doctor set his leg—though of course, Grace and her sisters had been forced to leave the room for that part.

"I would not ask it," assured Cook, "if it weren't for my knees. But . . ."

Grace suddenly felt very rude for even hesitating. "Of course I'll do it," she said, pushing back from the table. "There's no need for you to hurt your knees."

When Cook smiled, it had an almost mesmerizing effect. "Thank you, child."

Grace blinked away the odd effect, then said, "Cook?"

"Yes, Miss Grace."

"May I call you by your real name, the way Charisma does?"

Cook continued to smile. "My name is Euphrosyne."

Grace wasn't sure her tongue, though generally less clumsy than the rest of her, could manage that.

Luckily, Cook added, "But my friends call me Phronsy."

That, Grace could manage. "Thank you, Phronsy."

For the companionship. For the encouragement. And mostly for the chance to see Mr. Erikson again.

After all, Phronsy was right. As long as Grace used the dumbwaiter and did not actually try to serve Mr. Erikson the soup, what could possibly go wrong?

Chapter Three

The first time the child sneaked into his room, Jon thought he was hallucinating. He'd still been in pain, and Mr. Sullivan had some fine whiskey to offer as painkiller.

Besides, he'd been distracted by ungentlemanly thoughts about Grace Sullivan.

But the second time the boy appeared, Jon knew something else was going on—and he was ready for the little hooligan. He pretended to be asleep, though; all he'd been doing for the past two days was sleep, his shirt unbuttoned, his suspenders draped across the bedpost. He watched through barely cracked eyes as the little curly-haired boy slipped into the room, looked furtively about, then tiptoed silently to his bedside, surveying him with long-lashed interest.

Jon grabbed his wrist.

"Hey!" The kid leaped backward, ready to take flight, but Jon had a good grip and no intention of letting go. Jon was also considerably stronger than the child. After a few moments of twisting and turning, the kid finally stopped and scowled.

As if Jon, with his leg splinted and propped up on pillows, and his shirt unbuttoned halfway down his chest against the central heating of the Sullivan house, had been the one sneaking into and out of people's bedrooms.

"Let me go!" It came out slightly like "Letta me go." An immigrant kid.

A fairly gutsy immigrant kid, to judge by the way he'd lifted his pointed little chin and jutted out his lower lip. He stood barely taller than a hitching post, his wrist bird-thin, and he'd been caught red-handed. But he showed every sign of toughing it out.

"Not"—Jon gave the boy's arm a gentle shake, just to keep his attention—"not until you tell me what you're doing in here."

"Why? The Sullivans, they do not want you here, either!"

Not a half-bad observation. The only Sullivan Jon had seen since the doctor left yesterday was Paddy. Every time Jon heard a feminine voice drift past from somewhere else in the house, he'd sat up a little, hoping . . .

But it was a foolish hope.

"Whether they want me here or not, I've got an invitation. Have you?" Jon could tell from the boy's face that he'd hit on an interesting truth.

"Does it hurt?" asked the boy, his avoidance answering the question. As he eyed Jon's splinted leg raised on pillows, the child's big eyes grew wider in sympathy . . . and maybe some concern.

"This? Nah!" Jon shook his head, bluffing. "I'm a miner, kid. I've dealt with worse hurt in my sleep."

The boy looked impressed. Then he reached out and poked the splint. It felt like being kicked by a mule.

"AGH!" exclaimed Jon, letting go.

"You said it did not hurt!" protested the boy—though he did not miss the opportunity to take two quick steps backward. No slouch in the wits department, this one.

"Well, it didn't until you poked it," growled Jon. Only half true.

"I did not poke it, I touched it!"

"You poked it!"

"Did not!"

"Did—" It occurred to Jon that this was a less-than-mature way to handle the situation. It also occurred to him that the little boy hadn't run any farther; he'd just protected his ability to do so if he chose. "Do you even have a name?"

The boy considered him, a mix of wariness and interest on his little face. Then he grinned from beneath the hair. "I am Gio."

"Joe?" That's what it sounded like.

The pout returned. "Gio. *G-I-O.*" He seemed awfully short to know how to spell. Then again, he seemed pretty wily to be so short.

"Where are you from, Gio?"

"New York City." Again, Gio sounded proud.

"No, I mean what country."

"I am an American, you big Finn!"

"My family's from Norway, not Finland, and I'm American, too." Jon liked how the kid's expression changed with each new bit of information to absorb. "I'm Jon."

"The others, they call you Erikson." Gio had good ears, too. "That is a funny name. Are you Erik's son?"

"I guess sometime, long ago, one of my grandfathers must've had a father named Eric," Jon admitted. "But it's a perfectly good name."

"They also call you 'that dirt miner.'"

Now Jon scowled. "Who said—oh."

That would probably be Mrs. Sullivan. And he didn't know why he should take offense at it, whether she meant the term as derogatory or not. He *was* a dirt miner. Usually.

And damned proud of it. What other profession offered such adventure, such possible rewards? He was Fortune's companion! Destiny's beau! Wandering where the color led him, free and unfettered, his own—

"You will teach *me* to be a dirt miner, yes?" asked Gio hopefully.

What? "I will teach you to be a dirt miner, *no*," Jon told him. "You should be with your parents. What are they thinking, letting you wander around people's houses and sneak into strangers' bedrooms, anyway?"

"My parents are dead." The boy said it like an accusation, but his face showed pain, too. Oh. Well didn't *he* feel like a big bully.

"Sorry to hear that," Jon conceded, while the kid studied his feet on the carpet. Bare feet. And in the winter. "That must be rough."

"They worked very hard," said Gio. "But when Papa lost his arm in the factory, he was fired. Then Mama got sick, and the doctor would not come again without the money. I asked him and asked him, but he said he would call the police on me. Still I asked. But the doctor, still he would not come."

Oh, God. Stories like that kept Jon from ever,

ever working in a factory. Wage slavery—not for him!

Gio looked up from his little bare feet, suddenly very determined for such a short kid. "If we had money, the doctor would have come."

"You're probably right." Would it do any good to lie? "But your ma might have died all the same. My pa died, even with a doctor."

The boy nodded sympathetically, then climbed carefully onto the foot of the bed. Jon gritted his teeth, silent until the pillow under his hurt leg stopped shifting. Gio leaned his chin into his hands and said, "After Mama died, Papa brought me west so we could find opp-*opportunity*, and not be so poor anymore. But Papa, he got sick and died, too. In St. Louis, he died. I had no money to bury him, and the police put me in an orphanage, but I ran away. Nobody ever got rich being an orphan."

"But some orphans do get rich," Jon noted, both fascinated and confused.

Gio rolled his dark eyes impatiently. "This is what I will do. I will be an orphan who gets rich. Mining."

Oh. *Oh!* "Not with me, you won't," protested Jon. "I work alone. Footloose and fancy-free." He spread a hand in the air by way of illustration. "Fortune's companion."

Gio eyed him suspiciously. "You cannot have more than one companion at a time?"

Smart-mouthed kid. "Not if I don't want to."

Jon would have said more, except that suddenly Gio dived off, then under the bed, which again shifted the mattress and hurt his leg—right before there was a knock on the door.

Jon tried to peer over the side of the bed, but the

last thing he needed with this leg was to fall. "What are you doing under there?"

"Shhh!" whispered Gio. "They will put me out in the snow!"

Well, if Jon hadn't been sure about the kid's place in this house, he understood now. A stowaway.

"They will not put . . ." But then Jon considered Mrs. Sullivan's less-than-open-armed welcome of him. And he'd had an invitation, and saved her daughter's life. Or at least a limb or two. Oh, he doubted even *Mrs.* Sullivan would shove barefooted children out into a snowbank, but he didn't see orphanages as unlikely.

Maybe he should know more of the story before he made that big a decision. So he whispered, "Just don't distract me." Then he called a still-distracted "Come in?"

Grace Sullivan peeked awkwardly in and distracted him further.

The youngest Sullivan girl was just as pretty as he remembered—apparently, neither the pain nor the whiskey had colored that impression. She wore her pretty red hair pulled back from her face, but bits of curls escaped here and there. She had gentle blue eyes—not pale blue like his own but true blue, like the pattern on his mother's china. She wore a pretty green frock with some kind of stain on the hem, and she wore it well.

"Hello, there," said Jon, with his most winning grin. He'd been told he was handsome all his life. At first he'd just figured that was mothers and neighbor ladies for you. He began to believe it when girls started to tell him the same thing. He kind of hoped Grace would feel similarly. So he kept smiling as he asked, "How are you today, Miss Grace?"

She smiled back as if to say hello, but the words seemed to lose their way to her lips as she stared at him . . . and slowly started to blush.

Pinker and pinker.

Jon looked down at himself and realized what was amiss—his shirt still gaped open. "Oh! I'm sorry, ma'am. . . . If you'll excuse me for a minute . . ." And he began to button his shirt. It wasn't as if anything were wrong with his *hands*.

"I . . . I'll fetch your dinner," she said brokenly, her eyes still on his body. "I just thought I should open the door first. . . ."

Now *he* felt the start of a blush. "Yes, ma'am."

But his fingers slowed on the buttons as Miss Grace continued to stare at him, clearly fascinated.

She licked her lips, and Jon felt as if he were sinking even deeper into the bed's feather mattress. "Miss?" he prompted, and his voice came out more husky than he'd meant.

"Mmm?" said Grace, blinking.

He had the urge to start *un*buttoning again. Especially if the lady would consider obliging him with a similar unveiling. . . .

What was he thinking? Grace Sullivan was a good girl, the daughter of a family friend, *and* he had a tiny, too-wise orphan hidden under his bed. It wasn't the most auspicious time for such fantasies.

Assuming any time was a good time for such fantasies. "Um, Miss Grace? Ma'am?"

"Hmm?" Finally, Grace's attention lifted back to his face—and her blush finished its job. "Oh! Mr.

Erikson, I'm sorry, I . . . Dinner . . . Opening the door . . ."

She spun to flee and bumped into the doorjamb. *Uff da.* She righted herself and vanished from sight. Jon winced when he heard a thud outside in the hallway. "Miss Sullivan? Are you all right?"

"Yes," she called. "Thank—"

Something made a crashing noise as it broke.

". . . you," she finished weakly.

Jon had to take a deep breath to fight back the urge to go after her. The doctor had insisted he spend a week in bed before even trying crutches. Not that he could afford crutches.

Besides, he had to get his own reactions under control. He'd had women eye him like that before, sure. But who would imagine a *good* girl would look at him the same way?

A curly black head rose up by his elbow, on the far side of the bed from the door, and Jon glanced at the wide-eyed Gio.

"What is wrong with the nice lady?" the kid asked, awed.

"Nothing," lied Jon, looking back toward the door. "Not the least thing . . ."

"She has pretty shoes. Her ankles look very soft."

Now Jon looked away from the door. "Her *what?*"

"The shoe leather on her ankles. I think it is kid." Gio grinned. "Like me."

"You shouldn't be looking at a lady's ankles."

Gio shrugged, unconcerned. "Why does your voice get deeper when you talk to her?"

"Why are kids so annoying?" Jon finished buttoning his shirt. Yes, his voice had gotten deeper. And Grace had blushed. But this was not the sort of thing he planned to explain to a little boy. "You couldn't have mentioned the shirt?"

"It is a good shirt," said Gio, completely innocent to other issues. "For a miner."

Jon sighed and said, "Get down before she comes back."

Only then, as the kid vanished back under the bed, did he realize he'd just become the child's accomplice.

Only for now, he told himself. Only until he knew the whole story.

It wasn't as if little Gio would be wandering after him to any claims in the next month or two.

Grace sank into a corner of the upstairs hallway and hid her face in her skirted knees. Oh. *OH!* Could she have behaved more embarrassingly?

Not the falling down, or breaking the glass chimney from the wall sconce—that was normal for her. But *staring!*

Still, even as she remembered the horror of how she'd stared, she remembered the wonder of what she'd stared at.

He was so broad. And tanned. And he had hair like shadowy gold dust, especially where it sprinkled across his naked chest . . .

Just thinking about it confused her. She should be upset, but instead she felt flushed, even a little squirmy. She'd never known men looked so very nice under their shirts! She wondered if her older sisters knew; if so, the way they acted when they spoke of Misters Stanhope and Barclay would make even more sense. Except . . . surely neither Kit nor Will had chests like Mr. Erikson did . . . Could they? And even if they did, her sisters ought not to have seen them, just as she ought not to have seen this one.

Still, to think her sisters were entertaining their gentlemen in the parlor *right now*, made Grace blush. Only the thought that Mr. Erikson might be increasingly hungry, and was so helpless all alone in that big bed—rather, that big *room*—motivated her to regain at least some composure. All she must do was get his dinner from the dumbwaiter, take it to his room, and leave it with him.

Phronsy's assurances did not feel quite so powerful as they had in the kitchen. But surely Grace could do that much.

Besides, if she did not fetch the dinner soon, Phronsy might pull the dumbwaiter back down, see the food still there, and decide she must come upstairs to serve it after all. And Phronsy's knees hurt.

With new determination, and the hope that she was saving not one but two people from discomfort for once, Grace regained her feet. She futilely tried to smooth her skirts, then opened the little cabinet door in the wall, behind which sat the tiny, pulley-operated elevator platform. The soup crock was tied shut, she reminded herself after an extra moment's hesitation. And Phronsy had included extra napkins. She could do this.

With a deep breath, Grace clutched the sides of the silver tray and lifted.

So far, so good.

She carried it carefully back to Mr. Erikson's room, taking small steps. She did not dare look at him until she had set the tray carefully on the table beside him.

Success! And nothing had spilled.

After that, a shy glance toward his chest, only to find it neatly covered and buttoned, seemed an anticlimax. Or it did until Grace lifted her attention to Mr. Erikson's expectant face and beheld his smile. For a moment, she took encouragement from the fact that he looked not the least bit worried about the threat of a spill.

Only the realization that he did not know her well enough to be afraid diminished that encouragement.

"Thank you, Miss Grace," he said.

"You're welcome," she said. "Phronsy—that's the cook—she's the one who fixed it. I just watched."

"More than enough for any meal," he assured her, helping himself to the soup crock. "Is it all right if . . . ?"

"Oh, please," she said. "Do help yourself. Phronsy is a very good cook."

"I already believe that." His first spoonful of soup made him close his eyes in an appreciation that supported his words. Grace wondered if she could ever do something, cook something, that could give such pure pleasure to another person. Maybe to a handsome man . . .

She supposed she should leave now. Really, she should. Even with the door wide open behind her, this was a man's bedroom, and she had already seen his beautiful, gold dust-sprinkled chest once this afternoon. She ought not to risk scandal.

And yet her sisters were downstairs with their fiancés. As much effort as they and their beaux made to include Grace, she could not help but feel in the way during such visits. And Mr. Erikson must be lonely, too . . . musn't he? And she did like him.

He'd saved her life, and his hair made her think of shadowy mountain sunshine, and she liked him very much. So instead of leaving right off, she asked, "Is your, er, *injury* feeling better?"

Ladies oughtn't name body parts, after all.

"This?" He gestured toward the raised leg with his spoon. "I forget it's even broken."

Then he frowned, suddenly wary. "But don't touch it."

Touch his *leg*? She tried not to blush again. "I assure you, I won't."

"Are *you* all right?" he asked quickly. "That sounded like some fall you took."

"I'm fine, thanks to you," she assured him, twisting one hand in the other. "I hardly ever hurt myself."

Jon Erikson looked confused. He really did not know her. Grace marveled at the idea of someone not seeing her and immediately thinking of her as "Graceless Grace." That had to be why he'd smiled so broadly at her, not a hint of fear on his face. She longed for it to last forever.

But of course, it would not last. And he would be safer if he knew the truth. "I . . . I am not the most graceful person, Mr. Erikson," she admitted, embarrassed. "Actually, I'm rather . . . very . . . clumsy."

What Harold Latham had said last spring—that he'd "never seen anyone as *un*graceful as Grace Sullivan"—still hurt, even after months. Even after knowing how her big sister Belle had avenged the hurt.

"Call me Jon," insisted . . . Jon. "And I bet you're just modest."

Nice ladies oughtn't call gentlemen by their first names; Grace couldn't even refer to her future brothers-in-law as Kit and Will except in private family gatherings. And gentlemen were not supposed to refer to such vices as gambling, with phrases like "I bet," around nice ladies, either.

That Jon did both somehow felt like a breath of fresh air after the oppressive central heating roiling off the iron radiators in the winter, and Grace found herself smiling with true pleasure. "You're kind to say so," she assured him, "but I'm *terribly* inelegant. That's why I was climbing the stairs with a book on my head—"

"On your *head?*" he challenged, taking another spoonful of soup.

She nodded quickly, encouraged by how easy he was to speak to. The temptation to sit, in the chair by the window, was tangible. But that would not do. "To become more graceful," she explained, lingering by the bed table. "So that I can . . . can . . ."

So that she could win a beau as fine as her sisters' and make her mother happy. Somehow, that plan did not feel as worthwhile, telling it to him.

She said, "So that I can stop hurting people."

Jon dismissed her fears with another wave and a "pshaw," took another sip of soup, then said, "A little thing like you? Who could you hurt?"

"Mr. Erikson—" At his amused look, she boldly corrected herself. "Jon, then. I broke your leg!"

"No, *I* broke my leg. I stood wrong when I caught you, is all."

As if he caught falling women often enough to

expect a certain measure of extra competence in himself. If only it were true. But a history of dealing out black eyes and sprained ankles and broken crockery stretched behind Grace as far as she could remember . . . well, almost that far.

Since the family moved to the Little London of Colorado Springs, anyway.

Grace knew better. Still, she was hungry to hear differently. "You're just being kind," she told him, deeply grateful for it even so.

"No," he challenged, lowering his spoon and holding her gaze. His voice sounded deeper when he said, "I'm not."

His hooded gaze made her feel squirmy again. She felt an urge to lean closer to him, to see if his eyes were still so pale a summertime blue, half closed like that . . .

Then something—something clearly *alive*— brushed her ankle!

Grace couldn't help herself. She yelped, and she jumped to the closest safety, which was Jon's bed. Even as her elbow impacted the pottery crock, sending it flying, she knew she'd ruined everything.

Then suddenly, Jon had her caught around the waist with one arm, and he neatly snatched the flying crock of soup right out of the air with the other hand.

It sloshed a little, but nothing broke.

Grace stared at it, wide-eyed . . . still waiting, she realized, for the crash that inevitably followed such incidents. Then she looked quickly at Jon's very close face. His eyes were tightly closed.

His leg! She must have jostled his leg!

"Oh, I'm so sorry!" When she tried to climb

down, his arm tightened around her, so she sat still. "I'm so terribly sorry! I thought something ran across my ankle—I mean, my shoe, and oh, your poor, er, injury . . ."

"It's nothing," grunted Jon.

He did not sound very convincing.

"Then why are your eyes closed?" demanded Grace.

Jon opened his eyes enough to wince at her. "Really," he insisted, and showed his teeth in something close to a smile. "It hardly hurt at all. And it's not your fault anyway. It's the fault of *whatever's under the bed.*"

"Really?" Grace stared at him and realized she was sitting on the bed with him, and he was *holding her*—and she realized she liked it. She liked it very much. She felt safe with him, and practically harmless. "You caught the soup crock!"

"If I hadn't, you'd blame yourself," Jon reminded her, his voice deepening again even as it softened.

"You're wonderful," said Grace, and was rewarded with a smile.

Jon leaned closer to her, tightening his hold on her waist as he held her gaze. "So are you," he said, low and rumbly, and Grace thought he would kiss her for sure.

Then a little voice whispered, "Someone is coming!"

"Who said that?" asked Grace, sitting up to look.

Unfortunately, she was right on the edge of the bed, which she promptly fell off.

Chapter Four

Well, perhaps Grace Sullivan was a *little* clumsy.

Jon tried to hold onto her with his one free arm, but as she slipped from his grip he suddenly found his hand not on her waist but her ribs, then someplace soft and round . . .

Of course, he immediately let go, his hand burning with guilt—and she thudded to the floor. "Miss Grace?" he asked, putting down the crockery and looking over the bed's edge despite the pain of moving.

He caught a fleeting glimpse of the black-haired urchin slipping out the door. Then he noticed how Grace's skirts had ridden up to her knees, and his distraction was complete. She *did* have pretty shoes. And even prettier stockings. And absolutely beautiful legs.

With one impatient sweep, Grace brushed her skirts back over her legs. Jon forced his gaze back to her pouting face. "I told you," she said dourly.

"I'm the one who let go," he reminded her. Even if he'd had honorable enough reason.

He was rewarded by Grace's smile—just in time for the oldest Sullivan daughter, Belle, to appear in the doorway. "Hello, Mr. Erikson; I hope you're well. I know it's unseemly, but have you seen . . . ?"

Then she spotted her sister on the floor, and planted her hands on her hips. "Grace Sullivan! What could you be thinking, here alone with our guest?"

No questions about why she was on the floor. Just why she was alone in a man's bedroom.

"The door was open," defended Grace weakly.

Jon added, "She was just delivering my meal for the cook, Miss Sullivan." But of course, if one of her parents had found them alone together, even with Jon's bum leg, it might seem scandalous. That was something else Jon disliked about society. Society had to go and make rules instead of trusting individuals.

Although his guilty hand argued that maybe it *shouldn't* trust individuals.

"Well, next time think, for heaven's sake," insisted Belle, offering a hand. "Charisma and I have been looking for you. Comtesse Arabella has arrived!"

Comtesse *who*? For a moment, Grace—standing and brushing off her skirts—looked as confused as Jon felt. Then she perked up. "The connoisseur of feminine comportment?"

Feminine *what*?

"The very one," confirmed Belle. "Come along, now. Mr. Erikson, I'll send the maid to clean up that mess and to deliver future meals. I'm so sorry for the muddle."

"Wait a minute," demanded Jon, knowing full well that he was overstepping his place and, as usual, not really caring. "What's wrong with Miss Grace's, uh . . . comportment?"

The end of his question trailed off, though, because Grace—as if she had put them in charge of the discussion and turned to other things—was deliberately crouching down low, until she could lean her head almost to the floor and peek under the bed. Jon widened his eyes at her admirable sense of balance. This was the girl who thought herself clumsy?

Something did not make sense.

Miss Sullivan, perhaps wisely, did not deign to answer Jon's question. "Grace, whatever are you doing?"

Grace was already straightening but, perhaps startled at her sister's question, crumpled awkwardly onto the rug. "It must have run away."

Belle helped her up a second time. "What must have?"

"We're not sure," Jon said quickly. "Miss Grace thought something brushed her . . . *her*. Maybe a mouse?"

"Oh, dear," Belle sighed, though neither girl looked as upset about the threat of mice as he would have expected from ladies. Even his own sisters hated mice. "If you see any further vermin, Mr. Erikson, please do let our father know."

"I will," he promised, and watched, disappointed, as Grace followed her sister out to go see some *connoisseur* of *feminine comportment.*

But at least, at the last moment Grace turned and gave him a quick, secret wave.

Not two minutes after the sisters left, little Gio slipped back into the room, drew the door shut behind him—and went straight to Jon's silver luncheon tray. "That was a close shave, yes?"

"How is it they didn't see you?" asked Jon. The child, helping himself to a biscuit, only grinned with secret pride. So instead Jon scolded, "You touched her *ankle.*"

"The leather was very soft," admitted Gio, through a mouthful of bread.

So was the girl. Jon leaned back into his pillows and thought that this was going to be one long, lonely convalescence. Thank goodness he knew better than to depend on other people for his happiness. "As long as you're here, open the windows for a minute."

"It is freezing out!" protested the kid.

Exactly. Freezing . . . and fresh, and free. The mountain air was the one thing Jon knew could put even a pretty lady like Grace Sullivan in perspective. At least for a while.

And the way his fingers still tingled, Jon needed some perspective *badly.*

"Mr. Erikson is rather familiar," warned Belle as she preceded Grace down the stairs. "It might be better if you avoided him."

But Jon doesn't think I'm clumsy, thought Grace happily as she trotted after her oldest sister. One landing, two, then the foyer—no mishaps at all.

"You know how much store Mama places in our reputations," Belle added quietly—and with an odd note of irony—before turning into the parlor and raising her voice. "Comtesse Arabella, my youngest sister, Grace."

Grace entered the parlor, caught her toe on the edge of the oriental carpet, and sprawled into the midst of everyone. And it truly was *everyone*, she realized miserably as they surged forward to help her. Mama and Da were there, and Belle and Kit, and Charisma and Will.

And perhaps the finest lady Grace had ever seen.

Comtesse Arabella's travel suit was a confection as exquisite as anything Belle's dressmaker had created when transforming Belle into a beauty. Peacock blue cashmere trimmed with striped gauze, it was tailored tight to show the woman's small waist and then arched out into a generous bustle behind. More striped gauze spilled down the back of her skirt, like an elegant tail. Her hat, complete with real peacock feathers and more striped gauze, finished the outfit dramatically.

So this would be her fairy godmother. And yet, Grace noted loyally, the lady did not carry a fan. Belle had a whole collection of them; they'd recently become the ultimate fashion accessory. But the snowdrifts outside were taller than even Da. Perhaps fans were less appropriate in the winter.

"Does she often enter rooms like a racehorse?" inquired Comtesse Arabella of Mama, her accent nasal and crisp, while Grace was helped to her feet.

"Oh, no!" exclaimed Mama, patting Grace's shoulder nervously. "Not at all—that is, perhaps when she is excited to have such visitors . . . well, more often than not. Yes."

"Ah." Their guest spoke directly to Grace. "Do not bite your lip zo."

Grace realized she'd drawn her lower lip in under her front teeth. She immediately released it, then wondered how to hold her mouth. Lips completely closed? Slightly parted? Should she smile? Probably not.

She considered mimicking Comtesse Arabella's pursed lips but doubted she could make it look as natural. "Can you make me graceful?"

Comtesse Arabella walked slowly around her. Grace took hope from the careful study. Maybe the *comtesse* would see some simple flaw that her loving family had missed.

When she finished her circle, Comtesse Arabella said, "I will try."

Mama clapped her hands together in pleased relief. Da scowled.

"Perhaps we should leave you ladies to your new visitor," suggested Will Barclay, earning Grace's gratitude yet again by stepping into the awkward silence. "Stanhope and I mustn't overstay our welcome."

"You couldn't possibly," insisted Charisma, catching his hand between both of hers. Grace's middle sister had gotten better at swallowing back her more bald statements, but she still tended to speak eagerly when from the heart.

"All the same," agreed Kit, meeting Belle's amused gaze, "better that we err on the side of *not* being dreadful boors."

Then he bent and murmured something into Belle's hair. Grace's older sister nodded and smiled, clearly as pleased with her fiancé as ever.

This was what Belle and Charisma had managed in the half year since the three of them had made their wishes in the Garden of the Gods. Grace felt her own hunger for such happiness—such belonging—like an ache. *This* was why she must welcome her new teacher.

"And I've work to do," said Da quickly. "I'll see your luggage carried up to your room, Countess."

"Comtesse," corrected both Arabella and Mama at the same time.

"Comtesse," said Da politely, but secretly winked at Grace while he said it. He also patted her head as he passed her, as if for encouragement. But though Grace appreciated the love, she didn't need encouragement. She *wanted* to be elegant. Whether Jon Erikson, still upstairs in bed, thought she needed lessons or not.

The familiar sting of rug burn on her knees contradicted him.

The next week fell into a familiar pattern. Grace, always an early riser like her father, began her days before the sun rose, sneaking down to the kitchen's warmth to watch Phronsy prepare breakfast. She enjoyed the smells and the agility with which their cook moved from breaking eggs to mixing batter to heating water, almost like an intricate dance. If Grace was there early enough, Phronsy would ask her to deliver Jon Erikson's tightly wrapped breakfast before having her own.

Guilt at social impropriety warred with guilt at refusing to help an elder—and the latter always won. Grace knew full well that she oughtn't to be in a man's bedroom, certainly not while the man was in bed! The upset her parents had suffered, back when they'd discovered Belle in Kit Stanhope's hotel room, had shaken the household for several days. But truly, it had not made sense to Grace then, and it did not make sense now. Belle and Kit had only been talking; Belle had said so herself! Strange sayings about free milk aside, Grace simply could not make sense of some of society's rules.

In the same vein, she was only delivering breakfast. Mostly. And this was not even a hotel; it was her family's own house. That *had* to make a difference.

But just in case it did not, Grace found herself keeping one of her first secrets ever from her older sisters; she did not mention her charity to them. Since Belle and Charisma fell in love, they had not only social events to plan but private matters to discuss. *They* had secrets together.

Why should Grace not have one, as well?

Sometimes she had to wait outside in the hallway while Jon finished changing from his nightshirt into proper clothes. Something about standing just on the other side of the closed door, listening to a rustle of cloth or the snap of suspenders, made her feel wonderfully improper—but not enough to stop doing it. Once he called, "Come in," she would open the door wide, accept a smile of hello that warmed her far more thoroughly than Mama's central heating, and go to fetch the tray from the dumbwaiter.

Thus far, she'd spilled nothing on Jon since that first crock of soup—and even that, he still insisted, was the fault of the cat or rat or whatever had startled her from under the bed. Oh, she sometimes dropped the tray or tipped a plate off it. But between Jon's quick catches and the cook's tight wrapping, nothing spilled.

On top of everything else, Grace loved standing

just inside the open door and watching the big miner eat, drinking his coffee with solid gulps, wiping gravy or molasses from his plate with a biscuit the way Da did. He usually put aside a biscuit or pastry, perhaps for a midmorning snack, but often he would offer her a piece of bacon or a taste of bread, his eyes beseeching her to make him feel less like an oaf by accepting. She always did, even if it meant coming farther into the room. Sometimes their fingers touched, and his smile would widen, and she would feel surprisingly happy.

Grace hardly ever tasted the bacon or pastry that she obediently chewed and swallowed. She was too busy savoring Jon's smiles.

Not that she could stay through his entire breakfast, of course. All too soon the bell from downstairs would ring. She would take her leave from her miner friend and hurry downstairs to breakfast with her family. But not with Comtesse Arabella.

The *connoisseur of feminine comportment* kept what Da took to calling "noble hours," which meant she was rarely awake before noon. Usually, that was enough to set him and Mama at each other's throats yet again.

Mama generally claimed it a relief that the *comtesse* was not present to see how crudely Patrick ate his breakfast—gulping his coffee and wiping his plate, Grace noticed with growing discomfort.

Da insisted that since he dressed up for luncheon and dinner, he would certainly keep one meal of the day for normal eating. Then he would complain that Bridey had put Jon Erikson into a small third-floor guest room in order to reserve the larger guest room on the second floor for the countess. "And him with a broken leg!" Da usually exclaimed.

"She is a *comtesse*!" Mama would always insist right back. "She is *French*!"

Usually by then, Belle, Charisma, and Grace would escape the dining room to see to their own chores and plans. Mornings made for good sister time. But sometimes Belle and Charisma started to talk about things without really talking about them—holding each other's gazes extra long or stressing otherwise innocent words or phrases. "Did you and Kit find a little *extra time* at the opera?" Charisma might tease, making Belle blush. Or Belle would say, "Will does seem terribly . . . focused," and Charisma would smile and look quickly out the window. Then the silence would stretch out, and Grace realized she was somehow in the way. They wanted to talk about being engaged, and possibly about those invisible "lines" ladies were not supposed to cross.

When they first started doing that, Grace would try to dig an explanation out of them: "How can an opera have extra time?" or "Why is Belle blushing?" or "Isn't being focused a good thing?"

To the last, Charisma laughed and said, "Oh, yes, Grace. It is a *very* good thing!" But she still said it with that secret edge to her voice.

Was it so terrible for Grace, reluctantly granting her sisters their privacy, to take her companionship where she could get it?

Sometimes, if Da was not already spending the morning chatting with Jon, she would bring their guest a book from the library, or briefly open the window for him so that they could both breathe big gulps of the freezing mountain air, or talk about their families. Jon always sat up in bed to chat with her, as if it were not a bed at all. Grace always stood by the open door. But as long as his injury exiled him here, what else could she do to stay proper? Leave him alone?

Jon insisted that he did not get lonely, that she should not regret the time she had to spend on other matters. But Grace thought being left all alone must be the worst thing in the world, even if one *weren't* hurt.

When Da was already in Jon's room, Grace would find companionship in the kitchen, helping dry dishes—mainly the silver, which wouldn't break—while Phronsy washed them. Whenever Grace dropped a piece, Phronsy never seemed to mind cleaning it a second or third time.

"That is odd," murmured Phronsy more than once, looking at the towel where Grace had laid out the silverware. But like Belle and Charisma, the cook offered no further explanations of her veiled comments.

Then came the midday meal, a far more formal occasion, followed by Grace's lessons in elegance. Usually in the third-floor ballroom, she did a great deal of walking with a book on her head, with a broomstick tied to her spine, or with a length of rope hobbling her ankles to make her take smaller steps. Comtesse Arabella, counting out timing or calling out suggestions, had any number of clever tortures to force Grace into elegant lines her body resisted on its own. Despite it being time away from their fiancés' visits, Belle and Charisma faithfully took turns joining Grace. They balanced books, hobbled their ankles, and strapped on broomsticks, too.

"Someday I will be meeting Kit's parents," Belle reminded Grace gamely as they teetered about the ballroom together. "I'm quite sure I need help, too."

But Grace knew the real reason was so that she would not feel conspired against, would not feel like the broken wheel among them. She loved Belle and Charisma all the more for that effort, despite their having a secret code nowadays—and even if their efforts did not always succeed.

For Grace was terrible at her elegance lessons. Every afternoon brought a new disaster.

Comtesse Arabella tried to teach Grace and Charisma how to do embroidery. Grace realized immediately why she had never tried such needlework before. The silken threads were in beautiful colors and soft to the touch, but they tangled about her fingers and made her even clumsier. As the *comtesse* tried to untangle her, Grace stabbed the poor woman with an embroidery needle. Twice.

Comtesse Arabella suggested the next day that Grace and Belle try painting china, an equally ladylike pursuit that used less-sharp objects. Unfortunately, china became very sharp when broken, and Grace broke a great deal of it, then somehow tripped their elegant teacher into the midst of it.

Mama offered the *comtesse* more money after the doctor left, and the *comtesse* agreed to stay. Later that day, Da and Mama shouted about the foolish expense of it, and Grace felt guiltier than ever.

Clearly, she was not trying hard enough. But she had to make them happy somehow. She had to!

By the next week, Comtesse Arabella had the inspired idea of inviting Kit Stanhope and Will Barclay into the upstairs ballroom for dancing lessons. Both men exchanged glances of wary amusement—both had seen Grace dance—but for their sweethearts and their future sister-in-law, they bravely consented.

Grace stood by the wall, trying not to touch anything. That was one of the most repeated pieces of advice Comtesse Arabella had given her thus far: *do not touch!* She listened to Charisma play the piano and watched Comtesse Arabella and Kit Stanhope illustrate the most elegant of waltzes, and she wished with all her heart that she could do that. Grace loved music. She had been told, soon after moving to Colorado Springs, that ladies did not sing loudly to themselves as she'd been wont to do in Leadville, so she had taken to whistling secretly. Of course, ladies did not whistle, either, but it was easier to hide.

Listening to Charisma's music, Grace found herself swaying back and forth, hoping against hope that the *comtesse* would accomplish what, so far, nobody else had managed. She wanted to dance—not in happy spinning circles that made her fall down, but to really dance, with a man. She longed to become one with the music. She wanted to be truly part of a ball, too, not the element that disrupted it.

Perhaps she just wanted to be held.

Comtesse Arabella stepped back so that Kit could dance with Belle, and they, too, were poignantly elegant. The *comtesse* danced with Will Barclay, who somehow, with the sweep of the *comtesse*'s silken skirts, seemed even more competent a dancer himself.

"Now," said the *comtesse*, "who shall partner our little Grace?"

There was an awkward pause. Then both men stepped forward at once, somewhat more stoically than Grace would have preferred, but at least they did offer.

She ended up with Will Barclay so that Belle could continue to dance with Kit—which, to judge by how they held each other's gazes, was quite a treat indeed. Charisma played slowly at first, while Grace tried to hold her feet back to the appropriate patterns. While Will's presence or touch hadn't the effect on Grace that it clearly had on Charisma, he was a tall, handsome man and a pleasant enough partner. He, like Kit, would make a truly wonderful brother. Dancing with him was not terrible, though neither did it feel the way she imagined dancing should.

Dancing should feel big, and giddy, and dizzying, shouldn't it? It should feel . . . *free.*

Then, as Grace lasted through several minutes of that without doing damage, Charisma sped the pace toward something more like what they would hear at an actual ball . . . and Grace couldn't help herself. The music just felt so sweeping and dramatic, and Will was so terribly slow and careful. The piano music sparkling through her, urging her to truly *move,* Grace tried to draw him into bigger steps—

"Ze gentleman, he is ze one to lead," warned Comtesse Arabella.

Suddenly, Will was tripping over Grace's foot, and they crumpled to the hardwood floor in a heap.

The music stopped as Charisma hurried to her fiancé's side.

Will groaned. When Grace crawled backward, away from him, she hoped desperately that he would get up again. Most of her dance partners did, honestly! But when he sat up, he winced and bit back another groan—and held his ankle.

Oh, no.

Oh, no!

She'd hurt another one.

As if that weren't bad enough, a deliciously deep voice from the hallway said, "It looks like you could use this more than me, friend."

It was Jon Erikson, grinning at the chaos before him—and proffering a crutch.

Chapter Five

Not an hour earlier, Jon had been standing on one leg, holding the bedpost for balance and protesting yet more of Patrick Sullivan's generosity. "No, sir. It's too much."

"It's the least I can do for ye, boy," insisted Grace's father, extending the tall, T-shaped store-bought crutches. "Ye saved me youngest girl's life. I'll not be forgettin' it."

Oh, you just might. Jon also spent more time in that youngest girl's company, in this very room, than was anywhere near proper. Not that he'd tell the silver king that. It wasn't as though he'd done anything amiss with her, not since that first time when she jumped onto his bed and he'd felt her . . .

Well, that had been an accident. And other than that, they had just talked.

But Jon wasn't ignorant of those middle- and upper-class rules, all the same. His hometown in Minnesota had been full of them—yet one more reason he'd struck off on his own. He hungered for places where a man was judged based on his word and his abilities, not on following someone else's stupid rules that mostly boiled down to not trusting yourself or anyone else. He'd made no untoward advances toward Grace Sullivan, even when he'd wanted to. No deliberate ones, anyhow. If they were in a gold camp, folks would trust as much, or trust him to do right by her if the situation changed.

But this was Colorado Springs—Little London—and those foolish rules carried weight for folks like the Sullivans. Even for Grace.

It made her visits all the sweeter that she was risking so much.

Jon said, "I didn't do it for any kind of reward. You've already given me a place to stay, and good meals—"

"Ye mean to tell me ye value the meals over the ability to get around again?" The gleam in Sullivan's eyes said he understood Jon too well. Maybe there was still more dirt miner in Patrick Sullivan than there was silver king.

"No," Jon admitted, his hand itching to take the crutches. "I value that much more, which is why I don't want to be indebted—"

"Enough! I'm indebted to ye. Accept it, boy, and learn to use these things." Sullivan tossed the polished sticks onto the bed and turned to stalk out. But he stopped to look over his shoulder. "The man at the store said to be careful on the wooden floors. I'm thinkin' we could rig some leather boots for 'em, make 'em less likely to skid."

Jon looked at the crutches again. He'd been hobbling around a little, using the bed for support, but this . . .

One step closer to independence. So he swallowed his pride—and made a mental note to find out how much crutches went for, so that he could pay Sullivan back. "That's a good idea, sir. And thank you."

"Once ye've managed the stairs, I'd like to see ye at the dinner table." Sullivan shook his head. "I hadna' meant for ye to be hidden away up here like our crazy aunt. It's time we put an end to that."

His wife's likely reaction did not bode for the most pleasant of dining experiences.

On the other hand, Grace would be there.

"I look forward to it," said Jon.

Sullivan nodded and strode away. Jon picked up the crutches, adjusted them under his arms, took a tentative, swinging step toward the door.

Not bad.

He tried another one. His broken leg felt remarkably heavy with all that plaster, but he was a strong man; he could compensate for that. And he liked how his one booted foot thudded solidly on the floor now that he was ambulatory again.

Worth a hell of a lot more than the meals, he thought, shutting the door.

As soon as the latch clicked, little Gio clambered out of the wardrobe. Over the past week, the boy had taken to spending a lot of time with Jon. He ate food off Jon's dinner trays. He talked with Jon about hoped-for adventures and travels. Several nights ago he'd even appeared in the darkness, waking Jon up with sharp tugs on the sleeve of his nightshirt to say he'd had a nightmare.

Jon let the kid crawl onto that huge bed with him, and now the child was practically living there. *Only until I leave,* Jon cautioned more than once, and the boy always agreed.

But Jon had a bad feeling about it all the same.

He didn't like hiding the kid, for one thing. It felt almost as unfair to the Sullivans as to Gio.

"They have a crazy aunt?" The little boy's black eyes gleamed with excitement at that discovery as he hitched himself up on the bed.

"No, it's a saying." When one of the crutches tried to skid out from under him, Jon had to land quickly on his good foot to catch his balance. Simple. "He just meant, if they *did* have a crazy aunt, they might lock her up in the attic so that nobody would know about her."

Yet another example of upper-class morality, too often turned real. *Appearances are everything.*

"Like nobody knows about me." Gio nodded with more understanding than he probably had, and crawled across the bed to the side table, where Jon kept leftovers for him. This time he found a big, round cookie, another of the cook's treats, and sat dangling his bare feet while eating.

"No, not like you." Jon was getting the hang of this now, picking up a little speed as he circled the bed. "A crazy aunt wouldn't want to hide, which you do, and she'd be related, which you aren't."

He still hadn't learned much more of Gio's situation than hints that the boy had followed the cook here from Denver, supposedly without her knowledge. She had apparently fed him from her lunch basket at the train depot, and he'd liked the food enough to stay near her.

Gio, mouth now full of cookie, shrugged.

Jon stopped by the window, disliking his feeling of guilt. He rubbed a clear spot on the misted glass with his sleeved forearm to look out at the mountains, and felt a physical longing to be out there.

Not that a great deal of gold mining happened in the middle of winter—not above ground anyway—but, damn it, he hadn't struck out on his own just to end up trapped in a comfortable room with regular meals and a rapidly increasing debt to someone else.

Not to mention responsibility for a little boy that increased every day he kept Gio's secret . . . and fed him . . . and made sure he washed up. "It would be bad enough to owe them if they were family. But they aren't even that. Do you know what that makes us?"

Gio, still chewing, shook his head vehemently enough that his black curls bounced.

"It makes us charity cases. And if there's one thing I never meant—"

"Shhh! Someone's coming." The boy dived off the window side of the bed and hunkered down, lest the footsteps in the hallway stop at Jon's door. They didn't, which was probably just as well. It sounded as if there were too many of them—and several were fairly heavy—for it to bode well if they had.

"I don't like taking charity," Jon said, lower.

"It is all right," Gio assured him, climbing back up onto the bed as the footsteps moved on. "We will pay them back when we become rich miners."

"I've got news for you, kid. Very few prospectors really strike it rich." Then he heard what the kid had said. *Uff da.* "And there's no 'we.'"

Gio sat back, clearly startled. "Then why do it?"

Jon looked back at the moisture-smeared window, at the mountains beyond it. Because the mere hope of striking it rich justified the adventure—that was why. And the adventure was everything.

Piano music began to drift in from down the hall-way. The kid immediately scrambled off the bed and to the door, cracking it. "That is pretty!"

"I guess." It was a little too fancy for Jon, but then he had simple tastes.

"I'll go see what's happening." And before Jon could warn the kid to be careful, Gio had vanished. If Jon believed in such things, he'd swear the little boy could turn invisible. If he'd arrived at the same time the cook did, that meant he'd been here a good month, all alone, without anyone noticing him.

Jon hated thinking about that. It was one thing for a grown man to strike out on his own. Little boys should have someone watching after them.

Someone who wasn't him.

He went back to practicing with the crutches. By the time Gio slipped back into the room, Jon had learned to balance himself on just the wooden sticks, both feet off the ground. Once he accomplished that, he'd started trying to see how high he could raise his knees toward his chest before he had to put his good foot down again for balance. It was more tiring than walking was, but he'd been aching for the exercise, and his body savored the honest exertion.

The stairs were starting to sound easier and easier. Especially since, if he remembered right, the hallways and stairs had carpet runners.

With any luck, he would be dining with Grace Sullivan and her family this very night.

"The lady with the pretty shoes is there," announced Gio, as if reading Jon's mind. Then he said, "She is learning to dance."

"Dance to this?" But Jon was intrigued.

"With two other men, and her sisters, and the smelly lady." The smelly lady was the one Grace called Comtesse Arabella, who, apparently, wore heavy perfume. But the two other men . . .

"I'll go see." Jon swung his way out the open door and down the hall. His room was in a corner of the third story, and as he reached the archway at the other end of the short hallway, he found out why.

Most of the third floor opened up into a full ballroom, complete with tall, slim windows and a shiny wooden floor and a piano. In the middle of that space danced Grace and one of the men Jon had met that first day—Barclay, right? Stanhope was the blond man dancing with Belle.

Suddenly, Jon didn't like Barclay. For one thing, the man's stiff propriety annoyed him. Step-two-three, step-two-three, following an old and preordained choreography that, while it did fit the music, didn't necessarily have anything to do with this time, this place, or the woman in his arms. That was the main reason Jon disliked Barclay—the dark-haired man got to hold Grace, one gloved hand curled around hers, the other lightly cupping her waist. It might be proper dancing posture, but Jon felt jealous all the same. The weight of plastered bandages on his right lower leg felt heavier than ever.

Then Grace neatly yanked the fellow over, into a tangle of skirts and suit coat and groans, and Jon felt equally unattractive feelings: increased jealousy, since he knew what it felt like to sprawl with Grace Sullivan, and an ugly touch of glee.

Desperately he tried to go with his only pure

emotion—concern—but he had to readjust his crutches first. Charisma and Stanhope reached Barclay's side before Jon even crossed the threshold, so he swung to an awkward stop, noticing something disturbing.

Nobody seemed to be rushing to Grace's side.

Then again, Grace had quickly crabbed back from the mess and from possible assistance, clearly all right. She'd said something about not usually hurting herself, hadn't she? But Jon could tell by her wide blue eyes that she'd lied.

Grace Sullivan was in a great deal of pain. It just wasn't physical. And the more the rest of the room fussed over Charisma's fiancé, the worse it probably felt for her, too.

So instead of swinging to the rescue, Jon interrupted the fussing. "It looks like you could use this more than me, friend." And he extended one of his crutches.

It effectively drew everyone's attention off the injured man, at least momentarily. And it gave Jon a chance to be the one offering help for once—for the first time in a week—and not just the one who always had to accept it.

Grace looked up from where she crouched on all fours, and her face brightened to see him. Jon felt his whole self brighten in return, even if it was Kit Stanhope who—now that she'd stopped crawling—kindly helped Grace to *her* feet.

"Mr. Erikson!" Belle greeted him with a distracted smile—as the oldest daughter there, social niceties became her responsibility. Just because Jon didn't like following rules of etiquette didn't mean he wasn't familiar with more of them than he liked.

"How nice to see you up and about. Do you remember Mr. Stanhope and Mr. Barclay? And Comtesse Arabella, who is visiting? I'm afraid we've had a minor spill."

"Monsieur . . . Erikson?" greeted Arabella suspiciously. Jon could smell her thick floral scent from where he stood.

He nodded absently in her direction but extended his crutch again. "I noticed the spill. I can get by on one of these, really."

"No, thank you," insisted Barclay, waving away the offer as Stanhope helped him to his feet. He managed to limp toward one of a row of cushioned benches against the wall, grimly attempting a smile. "See? I'm perfectly well."

He clearly wasn't well, with that limp—not unless the man was a true weakling—but it was nice of him to pretend so for the ladies. The hope on Grace's face was poignant.

"That is enough of the dancing today," decided Comtesse Arabella, still looking Jon carefully up and down—and all but curling her lip. "Tomorrow, Miss Grace, we will review ze steps as you dance with a broom."

When Grace looked from Jon to the *comtesse,* the hope in her pretty face faded behind resignation. "Yes, ma'am."

"Perhaps we'd best be going, then," suggested Barclay, his smile tight. "Stanhope, would you mind . . . ?"

"Certainly, old boy." *Heaven forbid they borrow one of the lowly miner's crutches,* thought Jon darkly, edging back as the party made their way past him and toward the stairs. But that was unfair. They were probably leaving him the crutches more because of his broken leg than his low class.

But he *was* low class, which gave him certain freedoms . . . as long as he did not get caught. When Grace moved past him, chewing her lower lip and craning her neck to watch Barclay limp, Jon lightly caught her wrist.

Stay, he mouthed at her.

Her eyes widened. She looked over her shoulder at the retreating company, who were far more concerned with Barclay, then back at him, clearly torn.

Then she looked down at her wrist, so he reluctantly let go of it.

"Not for long," he promised, very low, so she nodded and waited, watching furtively until the others had vanished. But he noticed her rubbing her wrist.

He hadn't grabbed her hard. He *knew* he hadn't.

As soon as they were alone—except for Gio, who could be hiding anywhere—Grace spun back to him. "See? I told you, I'm terrible!"

"Not from where I stood," Jon assured her. "He's the one who was supposed to be leading you. Practicing with a broom may just be an improvement."

Grace's eyes widened, and she pressed a hand against her mouth to cover a guilty laugh. "No! Will's a wonderful dancer! You should see him and Charisma together."

Will. She had to struggle with her conscience to call him Jon, but her future brother-in-law was already Will.

"Then he's a wonderful partner for Charisma, but not for you. Was he afraid he would break you or something?"

Grace furrowed her brow, so Jon braced the knee of his broken leg on the bench beside him, propped his crutches against the wall, and held out his hand. "Come here."

Grace widened her eyes, afraid to move lest she somehow stomp on Jon's hurt leg or, worse, break the other one. Will hadn't been safe from her, and he'd had two good legs and advance warning about Grace. She mustn't risk her new friend.

"I couldn't." She shook her head.

He spread his hands and raised his eyebrows in a way that looked somehow roguish. That meant widening his summertime blue eyes. He had such pretty eyes and such a big, welcoming hand. . . .

"But your leg!"

"Trust me," he insisted solemnly, his voice deep and rich as ever. And she couldn't possibly hurt his feelings by not trusting him, could she? So Grace tentatively crept closer to him and looked up.

And up.

This was the first time she'd ever seen him standing. My goodness, but he was tall!

"First of all, if a fellow's going to hold a lady's hand, he should *hold her hand.*" Jon caught her right hand in his left, solidly enough that someone would have to make an effort to tug her away from him. His was big and callused and strong. She liked the way it swallowed hers. "And it's the man's job to lead."

"Will *was* leading," she insisted, unwilling to let even Jon think ill of a family member. Or an almost family member. "Or trying to. I don't think I let him."

"Well you shouldn't have had any say in the matter." Which would seem rude, except that Jon said it with a grin and distracted her. He not only settled a hand against Grace's waist; he pressed his fingertips firmly against her spine, one at a time, from his pinky up. Each point of pressure sent shivers through Grace until, by the time his index finger was settled, she felt fused to his hand. The heel of his palm on her ribs steadied her further.

Was that why she suddenly felt so weak?

"Now, relax," said Jon, and swung her to the right. With his fingers guiding her spine, she went easily right, all the way to the end of his arm's reach, which was far enough that her skirts swooshed around her ankles when he drew her back. Then he swept her to the left, his solid hand moving her as easily as if she were a rag doll. Again Grace's skirts swung satisfyingly past her ankles.

She loved this!

"See?" Before she even knew what he meant to do, Jon had dipped her backward, so that she was all but lying down in the air, balanced only on his big hand. With his other hand still holding hers, he rubbed his thumb in gentle circles on her palm. "All it takes is a little . . . uh . . ."

But for some reason, as his gaze lowered to her bodice—thrust up toward him because of how her back was arched—Jon seemed to lose track of the conversation.

"A little what?" asked Grace in a small voice, blushing up at him . . . and yet somehow intrigued, too.

"A little . . . confidence." Jon quickly drew her back up to her feet as if she weighed nothing, but left his hand on her waist. Grace felt glad he'd left his hand. She liked him touching her. "That's all. And a good jig wouldn't hurt, instead of that fancy ballroom music."

Now he was talking sense.

"Sometimes, when nobody's watching, I like to spin around," confided Grace. "Like I used to do outside, in the grass. Except that it makes me fall down even worse, and I don't need any help with that."

"Don't talk nonsense." Jon swung her back and forth again, as if they were dancing—except there was no music. And his feet weren't moving.

Hers were, and her skirts and petticoats were swaying, and she could easily imagine the music to go with them. "It's not nonsense, honestly!"

To her surprise, he let go of her waist, and she found herself spinning away from him, only to be snapped firmly back at the last minute by his hand on hers.

Now, *that* was fun!

"Maybe you're wrong," said Jon, spinning her neatly back toward him. But Grace couldn't catch herself in time, and he was no longer holding her spine, so she bumped nose-first into his chest.

His solid, chambray-covered, suspender-lined chest. He smelled of soap and water, and fresh air, and something else . . . something purely *him*. She suddenly remembered what he looked like without the shirt and suspenders, and the flush she felt had nothing to do with her dancing.

Then someone downstairs called, "Grace?"

And when Grace spun away to answer, she forgot to let go of Jon's hand. Maybe he *was* big. And maybe he was strong. But clearly, he wasn't used to Grace Sullivan.

"Whoa!" And he hopped quickly after her, to keep from being pulled over.

Grace froze, realizing what she'd done, waiting for the crash—but instead, both Jon's hands came down on her shoulders. For the briefest moment, she felt just what a heavy man he was.

Last time, *she'd* landed on *him*.

But now he was standing on his own again, behind her, using her shoulders to balance himself.

"I'm sorry," Grace whispered into the empty hallway. She was afraid that if she spoke too loudly, much less moved, he would fall down. "I'm so sorry."

"Don't be," Jon insisted, his voice a deep rumble against her back. He slid his hands down her arms but did not let go.

Did he have to hold himself against her like that for balance, or was he being forward? Grace wasn't sure she cared. Her eyes fluttered sleepily at the nearness of him, strong and solid like a Colorado mountain.

Then she glimpsed a bit of movement from a doorway. Short, dark-haired movement.

Jon's doorway.

Her eyes widened again. "Is there someone in your room?"

Chapter Six

"My room?" Jon's hands left her shoulders, so Grace risked turning. Sure enough, he was adjusting his wonderful new crutches under his arms. He swung neatly between her and the rest of the hallway—and his room. His eyes were extra wide and summery when she met his gaze, and his grin seemed oddly lopsided. "Uh . . . who would be in my room?"

Well how would *she* know? She supposed it could be Phronsy, come to fetch the luncheon trays despite her bad knees; Phronsy had black hair. Or it might be their day help, come to clean.

But the way Jon cocked his head, with strained casualness, made her wonder. "I don't know."

Again from below floated her summons. "Grace!" It sounded like Charisma.

"I'd better go," she said, circling him. "Thank you for the dance—" Her toe caught on something. Her body continued, though her foot was stopped, and she started to fall—with a clear view of one of Jon's crutches skidding down the hallway runner.

Then, instead of the inevitable crash and cries of pain, a strong arm caught around her waist and drew her back up. *"Uff da,"* said Jon softly—that funny word again—settling Grace back to her feet one-handed. "My apologies, Miss Grace. I'm, uh . . ." He lifted his one remaining crutch. "I'm still getting used to these things."

And he shrugged and widened his eyes in charming contrition. As if it had been his fault she'd kicked his crutch right out from under him.

Grace felt tears sting her eyes—tears of relief at how easily Jon Erikson seemed to be surviving their friendship. It had taken her sisters years to get as good as he was—assuming they were, even now. Her sisters weren't strong enough to catch her in midfall.

Much less to do so one-legged.

If she hadn't liked Jon before, she would now. But she *had* liked him, so now she outright adored him. She wondered if it was proper to adore a man this much. Particularly a dirt miner of whom her family would never approve, one who'd never offered to be more than a friend. Though why would he?

"You'd better go see what your sister wants," he prompted gently.

Grace nodded, backed away a step—and stumbled over his abandoned crutch. At least this time she didn't fall, which was a good thing, since he was too far away to catch her.

She crouched to retrieve it for him, but he hopped after her and put his other crutch on it. "I'll get that. Really."

Since she would probably just hit him in the head with it, Grace nodded and backed farther down the hall. "I'm coming," she called over her shoulder, toward the stairway.

Then, since she was right there, she glanced into

Jon's room. It looked the way it usually did when she delivered breakfast: the bed made, if a little messily; the wardrobe door cracked; the curtains open so Jon could see the mountains. Of *course* it was otherwise empty.

Was she imagining things?

"I'll see you at dinner." Jon's promise effectively distracted her, and she blushed to have been caught staring. It was his *bedroom*, after all. Where he *slept.*

And dressed.

Then she fully realized what he'd said, and gave a happy bounce. "You're coming down to dinner?"

He lifted his remaining crutch, reminding her that he could walk now. After a fashion.

"That's wonderful!"

"Grace!" Now Charisma's summons came from the stairway, clearly rising.

"I'll see you then," said Grace, and spun, and ran. She took the stairs at a happy gallop. Jon was coming to dinner. Dinner with the family. The way Kit Stanhope and Will Barclay often did! Almost as if he were courting her, although, of course, he was not. He was simply her father's guest, and a dirt miner at that. But still . . .

He was a guest who had danced with her, without music. One whose companionship she very much enjoyed in secret. Now she could enjoy it without the secrecy, too!

And Da was a miner. And Mama had let *him* court *her.* . . .

Not that Jon Erikson had made any move toward courting. Except for the dancing. And the smiles. And the friendship.

Grace wondered if she should ask her sisters how to tell when a man was just being friendly and when he was courting. But it had been easy for them. Their gentlemen had actually escorted them places. Even if Jon's leg weren't broken . . .

Charisma met her at the second-floor landing. "You needn't hide, Grace. Will's not angry at all; you know him better than that. He wants to make sure *you're* all right before he leaves."

Which was very nice of him, and they both knew it.

"How's his leg?" asked Grace as she fell into step beside her sister, hoping Will Barclay wouldn't need crutches. She doubted the lawyer could handle them anywhere near as well as the miner did.

"He'll be fine. Really." But Charisma's assurance held an edge of concern. She hadn't liked seeing Will hurt, and who could blame her?

Falling behind a step, Grace felt some of her joy from upstairs draining back into uncertainty. She didn't like seeing people hurt, either.

She liked hurting them even less.

In the alternate dimension that was Mount Olympus, Thalia shook her head. "You do know, dearest, that dinner may not go well."

That was the tactful way of putting it, and Euphrosyne, archetype of grace, knew it. But that was why Thalia got to be in charge of charm.

Still, Euphrosyne felt stubborn today. "My dinners are always perfect."

Thalia smiled. "I did not mean to insult the food;

you have always been a most gracious hostess, even disguised. I only meant that the company . . ."

Aglaia, resplendent in a trailing gold-trimmed toga of the finest white linens—pure classical, with nothing *neo* about it—said, "You know full well that Mr. Erikson cannot hope to please the girls' mother, much less that awful *comtesse.* He doesn't even have proper dinner attire. And"—she held up a beringed hand to stay Euphrosyne's protest— "while *you* may not see importance in that, Mrs. Sullivan will. And thus, so will Grace."

"Good." Euphrosyne folded her arms. "Perhaps she will learn to trust her own values instead of always defaulting to those of her family."

A certain amount of quiet self-assuredness was, after all, the hallmark of true grace.

Aglaia blinked, startled, but Thalia nodded. "Ahh. Clever, sister. I was wondering when you would do more for the child than send her about with breakfast trays."

"I do know what I am doing, dears." Euphrosyne noted how suspiciously Aglaia eyed her apron. Even in Colorado Springs, Aglaia had managed to avoid aprons. "I had plenty of time to plan this out while you two were arranging matters for Belle and Charisma. And you did set lovely examples."

"Then please do tell us," said Thalia, "what you have in store for that handsome young miner. He seems pleasant enough, but even if Grace learns to disregard her mother's wishes, I sense a certain wanderlust about the boy that could yet break her heart."

Jon Erikson was actually in his early twenties, but to immortals that put him in his infancy.

"Yes, dear," agreed Thalia. "He seems attracted to

Grace, and he has a good heart. But, as she is too dependent on her family's approval, he may prove far too enamored of his independence."

"Never fear, sisters," said Euphrosyne. "I've a plan for that as well."

Then she spoke words rarely uttered on Mount Olympus.

"Now I had best get back. My potatoes will boil over."

"I said no," insisted Jon, rubbing a sudsy rag up and down one bare arm, then the other, then under each, then across his chest. He'd warmed the water on top of the radiator, and he'd tucked flour-sack towels into the waist of his dungarees to catch the drips, but he still shivered as cold air washed over his wet upper body. "It's one thing to save left-overs off my tray. It's another thing to steal them right off the dinner table."

Especially since Mrs. Sullivan would probably be watching him like a hawk, just to make sure he didn't put his elbows on the table or tuck his nap-kin in his collar.

"But I will get *hungry.*" Gio sat on the bed with his chin on his knees, looking particularly big-eyed and forlorn, watching Jon bathe.

Jon tried very hard not to feel guilty. He'd done better by the kid than the urchin probably de-served. Far better than he should have, for Patrick Sullivan's sake. Jon was a guest in the man's house—had received crutches and a doctor's care—and still hadn't mentioned the little stow-away to his hosts.

"Which is why I should tell them about you, so that someone *can* feed you regularly."

Gio's eyes widened. "They will send me to the orphanage!"

"Maybe not." But Jon, splashing his washcloth free of soap, didn't need the kid's glare of cynicism to know he was a fool to consider otherwise.

The kid's cynicism just turned the knife, was all. "Or maybe they will," Jon admitted, drawing the rinsed rag across his arm. "But at least at the orphanage you'd have someone watching after you."

"*You* watch after me," protested Gio sulkily.

"Oh, no, I don't; I just . . . keep you company. I can't get you regular meals or a bed to sleep in." Not once *he* didn't have a bed, anyway. "Or shoes. Besides, I travel alone."

"You cannot send me to an orphanage!" Gio slid to his feet and spread his skinny arms. "You *cannot!*"

"Well, I'm not going to lie for you again, like I did this afternoon with Grace." That had felt horrible.

And he and Grace had been getting along so well this afternoon . . .

Now Gio's lower lip quivered, and his black eyes shone with tears of betrayal. Jon did not like this. He'd never volunteered to be responsible for anyone, especially not a seven-year-old orphan boy. All he'd wanted to do was keep a promise to his father by visiting Patrick Sullivan, then find someplace warm to hole up until the mountains thawed. And now that he'd gotten holed up in a mansion, with a stowaway he'd just . . .

Well, selfish though it was, he'd just been lonely. And bored. And it was hard *not* to feed something that cute.

Only too late was he now remembering what his mother used to warn him about feeding stray dogs: *They'll think they belong here.* Except this was worse, because this was a little person.

"I should have told them about you from the start," Jon admitted now, wincing at the truth of it. "And—and it wouldn't be me sending you to the orphanage, anyway. If Mr. Sullivan didn't protest, I wouldn't mind having you as a roommate for a few more weeks, until I head out. But he *would* protest, so that's just . . . that's just the way things are. You should be in an orphanage, where maybe some nice people can adopt you. You *are* an orphan."

Gio scowled. "And you are a big baby!"

Jon blinked down at him. "*What?*"

"You are a big coward," insisted Gio, with a decisive nod. "You worry what the rich people will think of *you*, but they do not care what you think of *them*."

Good try, kid. Jon untucked a towel from his pants and began to dry himself off with sharp sweeps of cotton. "Grace Sullivan cares."

She came to see him every morning, and she talked with him about the mountains, and today she'd pretended to dance with him, even if he was currently a cripple. She'd confessed to spinning around until she fell down—fell down for normal reasons—as if it was a secret she'd shared just with him. The more time Jon spent with Miss Grace, the more he thought she did care, just a little. At least as much as a friend would.

"She does not care," said Gio, pouting.

As if the sprout knew women. "Yes, she does."

"No, she does not."

"Yes, she—" Jon caught himself, narrowed his eyes.

"And even if she didn't, that doesn't make it all right for me—for us—to keep secrets from our hosts."

"The rich man, he would not care, either," insisted Gio. "He hates his money, his fancy house. He said so."

Jon reached for his clean shirt. "He's never actually said that to me." But Sullivan didn't seem particularly happy with his wealth, either.

"He's said it to Mrs. Rich Man."

And if anyone could have overheard it . . . "Their name is Sullivan, and you shouldn't listen in on people's private conversations."

Gio widened his eyes, suddenly helpful. "If I promise not to listen, will you still hide me?"

Jon groaned.

"It is only for a few more weeks," insisted the boy, ducking his head now, coaxing. "You said so yourself. And Mr. Sullivan, I think he would not mind if he knew. Only his wife would mind. They . . . they might even fight about me, if you tell. That would be your fault."

"Because otherwise those two would never argue about anything," said Jon dryly, shoving his arms into his sleeves.

"And it is very cold out," Gio reminded him, nodding toward the window. Jon couldn't see the mountains for the snowfall this evening. Would spring never get here? "Maybe the orphanage cannot afford coal like the Sullivans can."

"Spare me." But the damnable part of it was, the child could be right.

"Or enough food." Gio's eyes seemed bigger by the second. "And maybe they beat little boys."

Jon pointed at him, wary now. "That's not fair."

"They beated little boys at the St. Louis orphanage. With a big stick. They told me so."

Jon groaned, unsure what to do with all the mixed guilt tightening up his throat and chest.

Gio blinked, all innocence and quivering lip. *"Please?"*

Jon began to button his shirt. "Look, I have a dinner to go to, and a connoisseur of feminine comportment's gonna be there. I don't need to be worrying about this right now."

Gio ducked his head, slanting his eyes upward in a silent—and even more powerful—*please.*

And Jon just couldn't do it. "So how did you manage to eat before I got here?" he asked. It wasn't as if he wanted the boy to go hungry.

He didn't expect the kid to hurl his small self at him, wrap his skinny arms around his waist, and bury his curly head against his shirtfront. It made him feel even guiltier. And still wrong. And somehow, as he reluctantly patted the little boy's back, marveling at such fragile bones, Jon felt something else. He felt strong and wonderful.

He knew better than to trust that last part. He was keeping quiet because he'd kept the secret too long to disentangle himself now; that was all. He was keeping quiet because he cared too much what Patrick and Grace Sullivan thought of him, even if he was deceiving them into those beliefs. And he was keeping quiet because he did not have the heart to make a little boy cry by doing the right thing.

Gio was correct. In this matter, at least, Jon was a coward. Certainly too big a coward to take on responsibility for anybody other than himself.

* * *

"Belle!" Grace peeked out the cracked door of her bedroom and looked in both directions to make sure no menfolk were around. Though near tears, she felt fairly certain everything was clear. Then she scurried from her room to her big sister's, wearing only her underwear and petticoats, her arms full of pale blue evening dress. She knocked once, thought she heard something from the stairway, and ducked inside.

Unfortunately, she closed the door on part of the dress she carried. When she hurried deeper into the room, the gown was wrenched right out of her hands. *"No!"*

She had to spin back, open the door long enough to free the dress, then close the door again. Then she studied the gown, looking for signs that the door—or the wrench—had done even more damage than usual.

"Grace?" Belle sat at her vanity table in her own underwear, a powder puff in her hand. But she was only applying a little talcum—Grace could tell by the sweet smell of it. Belle had learned her lesson about cosmetic powders.

Grace thought Belle looked nicer with freckles anyway.

"It isn't right," she said, dropping the rustling pile of netting and silk onto Belle's neatly made bed. "I tried to put it on the way the dressmaker did, but it just isn't right. I wish Madame Aglaia were still in town."

When Madame Aglaia had helped create new dresses for Belle, every one of them had somehow reflected the true beauty of Grace's oldest sister. But the gowns that Mama and Comtesse Arabella had ordered for Grace, from the best remaining dressmaker in town, seemed to have the opposite effect.

"Let me see." Belle left the vanity to come to the bed and spread out Grace's gown properly. "The blue one? Are you sure you don't want to save it for the lyceum this Friday night? Several nice gentlemen are going to be there."

Not as nice as Jon. But when Grace even considered saying that, her voice faded away to nothing. She wasn't sure she should confess her feelings to Belle just yet. Belle had already suggested she stay clear of the "familiar" Jon Erikson. She might tell their parents, who might give orders.

And if ordered to stay away from her friend, Grace would have to do it if only to preserve what remained of the family peace. Wouldn't she?

Better to keep her secret. So she cleared her throat and said, "I thought perhaps I should try wearing it first. At home. Where it doesn't matter so much if something goes wrong."

Except that it did matter. Jon was coming to dinner.

"I suppose Mama will be pleased that you're joining her and the *comtesse* in dressing up, but dearest . . ." Belle hesitated, drawing her mouth to one side, then just came out and said it. "Are you certain you want to risk ruining this before it truly counts? I'm afraid your gowns don't last very long."

But tonight *did* truly count. "I'm certain," Grace insisted. "But it doesn't look right, and I don't know why."

"Then let's try it on you." And Belle slid it over Grace's head with a rustle of weight and fine material. Grace felt herself relaxing immediately; now that Belle was helping her, everything would sort itself out.

Where would she be without her older sisters?

"One problem is that your corset isn't tight enough. Hold on to the bedpost . . ." And Belle tightened Grace's corset strings in strong pulls, while Grace did her best to suck in her tummy and hang on to the wooden post until she felt Belle drawing the bodice of the dress back up. "There. That should help. Now . . ."

Grace looked over her shoulder, into Belle's vanity mirrors. "It's still awful. It has all these . . . these *things* on it." She sharply brushed at a silk flower with ribbon leaves, increasingly grumpy. She doubted Jon would like a dress with all these fake flowers on it. She imagined he liked real flowers, as she did—if he liked flowers at all. "And it sags in back. It didn't sag at the dressmaker's."

Suddenly, Belle pressed a hand over her mouth, too late to stifle her quick laugh. "Oh! Grace, we forgot your bustle!"

Her . . . ? Oh. Grace remembered the contraption of metal bands and leather straps back in her room. First they'd been in style. Then they weren't. Now, according to Comtesse Arabella, they were back in. Who could keep up with such things? She supposed that once she had that on, the rear end of her dress wouldn't sag nearly as much at that, and she sighed. "Being elegant is certainly a lot of work."

"Oh, but it's worth it," Belle assured her with a

kiss on the cheek, going back to her dressing table. "When the right man looks at you, and you realize he's really looking at *you* . . ."

Her gaze dropped to her engagement ring, and she sighed happily.

Grace thought about Jon's summertime blue eyes, and how unfocused and sleepy they sometimes seemed when he looked at her. It made her shiver when he did that.

"Is that how you know?" she asked. "When he looks at you a certain way?"

Belle started to brush her hair but caught Grace's gaze in the mirror. "How you know what?"

"That a man is sweet on you."

"Oh. Well . . . I suppose the best indication of that is when he asks to pay call." Belle narrowed her eyes, suddenly thoughtful. "Why? Do you suspect there's a gentleman who might soon be paying call on *you*, Grace Sullivan?"

A *gentleman?* Not exactly. Not in the same way Kit Stanhope and Will Barclay were gentlemen.

Grace's voice disappeared again, so she just shook her head.

"Well, don't you worry," Belle assured her. "Spring will be here soon, and then there will be far more parties and picnics, and you won't have to hide your pretty clothes under heavy coats. You'll meet the perfect young man, and Mama will be thrilled, and Papa will see that she hasn't hurt anything with her worries, and all our wishes will have come true. You'll see."

Grace hoped so. She'd had an image of herself being escorted on the arm of a proper upper-class fellow, along with her two sisters and their beaux, attending the opera or one of Mrs. Bell's social events, with Mama and Da looking on and smiling. The family would be happy again. Perhaps all three sisters could have homes built on the same street, and they could be together always.

It was a fine future to imagine, except for one thing.

Grace did not care a fig about the faceless, imaginary man who could give her such a nice house, and operas, and social events.

She would rather stay home and talk about the mountains with a friend like Jon.

One whose eyes made her shiver.

Chapter Seven

Jon managed the stairs with a series of smooth hops, his crutches in one hand, the banister firmly braced under the other. One flight, and a landing. Another flight, and a landing. Between his injury and a week of forced immobility, he felt a bit winded, but it was no harder than hiking in the mountains. Getting back up might be a challenge, but after a week his body longed for more physical challenges.

Then, on the last slant of stairs, he looked up from the steps beneath his feet, saw Grace with her two sisters at the foot of the stairs, and had to pause lest he stumble. Grace was that pretty.

Odd. Jon had stepped out with prettier girls before. Not as wealthy, maybe—to a man who was Fortune's companion and Destiny's beau, a lady's wealth could be seen as a shortcoming. But taller girls. Blonder girls. Girls far less likely to accidentally injure him.

So why could the memory of none of them hold a candle to the hopeful, upturned face of Grace Sullivan? Why did his heartbeat speed up around *her?*

He guessed it was because when he looked at her,

he saw more than coppery curls, more than a wide, friendly mouth, more than cream-fresh skin. He saw a lot more than a fancy blue dress with fake flowers sewn to it—although it was a fine dress, and Grace looked particularly curvy and feminine in it. What he saw was the friendly face that had made him feel at least partially welcome in this tall, over-heated house. He saw her wonderfully gentle spirit. And in her tentative smile he saw one more thing— something he began to recognize only because of his failure with little Gio.

Grace seemed to need him.

Well, to need *somebody* anyway, he thought quickly. It didn't have to be him. *Shouldn't* be him. But she seemed lost nevertheless, overwhelmed by fine clothes and fancy manners and crowded knick-knacks.

Starting down the last flight, Jon paused one more time to squint at a shelf full of pastoral fig-urines beside the stairs. Was that an *arm* in the porcelain milkmaid's pail?

"Good evening, Mr. Erickson," said Grace for-mally as, thoroughly distracted now, he reached the bottom and readjusted his crutches. Jon liked it better when she greeted him in his room, called him by his first name, but, of course, with polite company around them . . .

One more reason Jon disliked polite company.

"Yes, good evening," her oldest sister said.

The middle sister said, "I hope you are mending well."

"As well as can be expected," Jon assured them, fa-voring all three Sullivan ladies with a grin. "I hope the same can be said for your fiancé, Miss Charisma?"

To his delight, Charisma Sullivan grinned easily back, more like a regular woman than a rich one. "Mr. Barclay will be fine, thank you. I'll tell him you asked."

"I didn't figure Miss Grace could do too much damage," he said. All three sisters tried valiantly not to look down at his broken leg. Only Belle succeeded. "Unlike clumsy types like myself," he added, catching the prettiest gaze in the room with his own. It took all his questionable manners not to wink.

Grace's gaze brightened back at him. Then, wink or not, she blushed and looked down, softly biting her lower lip. But it was a shyly smiling lip she bit.

He felt strong and wonderful again.

He suspected he might regret that feeling.

"It's good to see you up and about," said Belle, also without a sign of snobbery. Maybe it ran in the family. They *were* only first-generation rich. "Perhaps now you can join the family for games in the parlor, of an afternoon."

"I'm certain Mr. Erikson has better things to do with his time than spend it with young engaged couples," someone chided from the landing, and all of them looked up to see Mrs. Sullivan descending the staircase with Comtesse Arabella holding her arm. Both women were dressed even more formally than Grace . . . and neither seemed pleased to see Jon.

Perhaps the girls simply took after their father.

"True enough," Jon agreed into the momentary silence that followed Mrs. Sullivan's pronouncement. "I don't suppose sweethearts ever get enough time alone together when they're courting."

He had to fight the urge to look at Grace as he said that. Not that she was his sweetheart, really. But he did appreciate their time alone. He appreciated it a lot.

Because he wasn't looking at the daughter, he noticed that the mother seemed flustered by his words. Her gaze darted past her older daughters before veering away.

"So is it almost time for dinner?" asked Charisma quickly.

"I believe we are having pot roast tonight," Belle added, just as rushed.

Now Jon did look at Grace, who met his gaze with equal confusion before looking from one sister to the other.

"Why does everyone get so nervous when we talk about you spending time alone with Kit and Will?" she asked.

Comtesse Arabella cleared her throat, and Grace said, "I mean, Misters Stanhope and Barclay."

"Nervous?" asked Belle, with a here-and-gone smile that, to Jon, looked purely nervous.

"Don't imagine things, Grace," said Charisma.

Grace's brow furrowed until she met Jon's gaze again. He widened his eyes deliberately at her. If she was imagining things, so was he.

Her brow smoothed, and she smiled at him as if he'd helped, just by being there, just by hearing what she had.

Jon loved her smile.

It made him feel strong and . . .

Uff da.

Grace thought Jon looked wonderful. His gray frock coat had none of that starched, off-putting stiffness she usually equated with men's suit jackets; instead it looked worn and soft, and it strained slightly across his back, which seemed a fine testimony to his shoulders. His dungarees looked soft, too, and he'd polished the boot on his left foot, though, of course, his lower right leg was encased in white plaster. She hadn't seen his dress shirt, more or less white after who knew how many washes, but she liked how it looked without a collar. Most men nowadays used disposable collars of paper, or even a paperlike material, which were rumored to burst into flame too easily for her comfort.

In fact, everything Jon wore seemed sturdy and washable. If allowed, she could get as close as she wanted without undue worry. Grace loved that. She loved how tall he stood, even with crutches, and how easily he smiled.

Which was why it so surprised her when Comtesse Arabella, passing him, simply looked him down, then up, then looked deliberately and silently away.

Luckily, Da came hurrying down the stairs then, still buttoning his finer, stiffer coat. "Erikson! Good to see you up and about. How are those crutches working for you?"

"Very well, sir," Jon assured him, showing dimples again. "I'll be out of your way before you know it."

The words, no matter how rich and deep his voice, echoed like a shriek in Grace's ears. He was leaving? He'd barely gotten here, and he was leaving? He couldn't leave. He *mustn't!*

But with her sisters and her parents and her connoisseur of feminine comportment looking on, how could she protest? The words choked up and hurt, hard, in her throat.

"Not at all, not at all," said Da for her. "Stay as long as you like. It's good to have someone regular to talk to. Well, Bridey, I could eat a pack mule. Shall we go in?"

"Ladies first," said Jon.

See? He was no ruffian.

But by the way Mama and Comtesse Arabella glanced past him as they walked by into the formal dining room, he might as well have been.

Grace hoped to sit across from Jon, so that she could watch his pretty eyes, but something better happened—she got to sit beside him! Mama and Da, of course, sat at opposite ends of the table, and Mama had Comtesse Arabella to one side of her, Charisma to the other. Da had Jon to one side of him, Belle to the other. That left Grace to sit either between her sisters or between the guests, and the extra chair was set between the guests.

Jon pulled her chair out for her, competent despite his crutches. Grace hoped, when she smiled up at him, that everyone at the table couldn't see how pleased she was.

When he glanced to make sure nobody was watching, then quickly winked, she feared it might be a lost cause. It had been a long time since she'd enjoyed family meals, considering how often the family argued nowadays. But she thought she would enjoy this one.

Especially since she'd helped prepare the meal! Phronsy had allowed her to crumble herbs into the soup and to knead dough, earlier this afternoon. Grace had enjoyed it. Dough was *supposed* to be dropped—as long as one only dropped it on the counter. She loved the pliable feel of flour between her fingers, the smell of the herbs on her hands. Now . . .

"Thank you," said Jon when Phronsy placed a bowl of soup in front of him. He politely waited until Mama started eating—again, no ruffian—before trying it himself.

Grace held her breath.

Jon closed his eyes for a moment's pleasure, then opened them to smile at Mama. "Excellent soup, Mrs. Sullivan."

Grace felt a warm thrill go through her, as if his pleasure were hers. She wondered if she should mention helping.

Mama said, "Cook does very well, thank you."

"Her name is Euphrosyne," said Charisma. "Considering how many people call any Irish domestic Bridget, no matter her name, I hope we of all people can set a good example by using our help's real names. Even if they're Greek."

"We of all people?" Mama used her frosty voice.

From Belle's odd sideways movement, Grace suspected her oldest sister had just kicked Charisma under the table. Charisma narrowed her eyes in response. Here it came. . . .

"Yes, Mother," said Charisma, her chin high and her shoulders set. "Being Irish."

"I hope, young lady, that you are not categorizing us with scullery maids and factory workers! Not a person at this table was born in Ireland, praise the Lord."

"But our grandparents were," said Charisma. "And I see nothing shameful about admitting it."

"You'll speak respectfully to your mother," chided Da, then softened the rebuke. "Though you're correct—there's not a thing shameful to being Irish."

"Nothing shameful?" Mama put her soupspoon down with a clank. "Tell that to the shopkeepers who put cruel signs in their windows: *No dogs or Irish allowed.* Tell that to Denver's Sacred Thirty-six!"

"Their foolishness need not be ours," said Da.

Mama opened her mouth, then shut it firmly, wincing toward Comtesse Arabella—who was politely eating her soup and staring off into space. Grace did not think the *comtesse* had kicked Mama under the table, but she might as well have. "Enough. I will not have this disagreement in front of our guest."

Da cleared his throat, and Mama flushed.

"Our *guests*," she corrected between her teeth.

"I apologize if I was disrespectful," said Charisma, far more easily than she ever would have before she'd met Will Barclay and the widow Pappadopoulos. "I only meant to request that we call our cook by name. Euphrosyne."

"Would that we could," mourned Da, with a comic sigh. "But I can't seem to fit me mouth around it."

Grace said, "She doesn't mind being called Phronsy, either," which earned an approving glance from Charisma.

"Surely," said Mama, her voice increasingly tight, "we can discuss more elevated topics at dinner than how to address our immigrant cook."

Jon grinned and said, "We could discuss Pikes Peak."

Da laughed, and Jon chuckled, and Grace finally got the joke. *Elevated.*

Mama scowled both men into silence.

But at least, Grace then got to watch Jon savor every drop of his soup—and two pieces of the bread she'd helped make—before they moved on to the next course. She wondered, as he dug happily into his pot roast, if Phronsy would let her help with the entrée tomorrow.

Watching men eat was even better when she'd helped prepare the food.

The conversation was nowhere near as savory as the dinner. Da brought up the possibilities for mining copper once the silver began to pan out, which Jon seemed to favor—but Mama reminded them that it was rude to discuss business at the table. Comtesse Arabella told Mama about some of the delicacies she'd been served at the French court, but Da made a derogatory noise at her description of snails in garlic butter, and she pointedly let the topic wane. Belle told Charisma what she'd heard about the topic for Friday evening's lyceum, down at the schoolhouse—it would be another debate, this time over the Society for the Prevention of Cruelty to Children, and Charisma loved debates. But when Belle asked if Robert James would be there, perhaps would even insinuate himself into their party in order to get closer to Grace, Grace was the one who felt uncomfortable.

For one thing, Mama said, "Of the *Denver* Jameses?"

And for another, she sensed that Jon was watching her after that. She didn't dare look to see if his attention was relieved, surprised, or disapproving.

"I doubt Mr. James has his eye on *me*," she protested softly. They'd only spoken a few times. The family seemed to think the fact that she had not yet spilled anything on him, knocked him down, or set him on fire meant he would soon be in love with her.

"Don't be so sure," teased Charisma.

Jon said, "Why wouldn't he?" As if a man would be a fool *not* to have his eye on her. So she peeked up at him after all.

He looked troubled but defiant. He'd meant it.

Mama said, "There are certainly things you can do to draw his eye, Grace. Ladylike things, of course."

As opposed to knocking someone into the punch bowl, or falling and ripping his coat clean off. Grace sighed, unhappy even to *think* about the lyceum this Friday.

Then, halfway through dessert, Mama startled everybody when she said, "Charisma, may I see your spoon?"

Charisma blinked at her mother, amused. "Excuse me?"

"Your spoon," repeated Mama. So Charisma passed over her utensil. Grace looked at her own spoon, wondering.

Mrs. Sullivan looked at it, lifted her own spoon, then compared the two. Then she put down both, picked up the bell beside her, and rang it. Loudly.

Da said, "For the love of mercy, what is it now?"

In the meantime, Comtesse Arabella bent to peer more closely at the silverware. "Why, Marie, you're correct. How very embarrassing."

Mother liked to be called Marie, after her middle name, which actually was Mary.

"What's embarrassing?" asked Grace, now looking at Jon's spoon. He offered it to her for closer inspection. Somehow, in taking it, she caught her thumb on the edge and launched a glob of pudding toward her father—but Jon snatched it out of the air before anybody even noticed. Then he wiped it off his hand with a napkin, under the cover of the table, grinning broadly.

Grace blushed, suddenly wishing dinner were over.

"Whatever is the matter, Mother?" asked Belle.

Charisma, still spoonless, sat back in her chair and waited.

Phronsy appeared from the kitchen, drying her hands on an apron. "Mrs. Sullivan? Are you finished with the pudding already?"

"Cook," said Mama sternly, "the silverware does not match."

And the room fell momentarily silent—in confusion.

Da said, "Jesus, Mary, and Joseph. Is *that* what you've got your dander up about?"

Jon held his spoon next to Grace's, then shrugged. She couldn't really shrug in a corset, but she agreed. *Theirs* matched.

"No, ma'am," said Phronsy after a moment went by without her being asked an actual question. "They do not."

"We should have enough of this design to serve eight, should we not?" demanded Mama.

"Mother, please," murmured Charisma.

Phronsy said, "Yes, ma'am. We should."

"I only count seven people at this table," said Mama. "And the flatware does not match."

Da shook his head. "For the love of Mike!"

"Yes, ma'am," said Phronsy. "I had hoped not to bother you with this until I was certain, but . . ." And she took a deep breath. "Mrs. Sullivan, some of your silver may be missing."

Worse, Mama looked directly at Jon when she said, "Oh, is it?"

Jon honestly had no idea why Mrs. Sullivan was giving him the evil eye, not even when Grace's mouth fell open in a gasp of protest.

Then Patrick Sullivan leaped up, and chaos ensued.

"Ye'd best not be thinkin' what I see you're thinkin', Bridey Sullivan," he warned, even while Charisma said something like "Mother, really," and Mrs. Sullivan shouted something like "Do not raise your voice at me, sir!" and the cook—Phronsy?—said something conciliatory, and the perfumed *comtesse* said something nobody could have heard anyway.

Mostly, though—what with his sitting right next to him—Jon heard the man of the house. "This here is a trustworthy fellow from a trustworthy family," insisted Patrick, thumping the table with his fist for emphasis. "And when would he have found time to do this thievin', having just gotten his crutches today? I'll not sit by and watch you disparage a fine young man like this one, much less a guest!"

"Me?" By then, Jon was figuring it out. It seemed

almost redundant to protest his innocence, with Sullivan shouting like that, but Grace sat on Jon's other side, eyes wide with dismay, and he could think of little worse than her believing this. "I never stole anything in my life!"

"And who would you blame?" demanded Mrs. Sullivan of her husband. "*My* guest?"

This time, Jon heard the *comtesse*. "Really, Marie."

"I only noticed it a few days ago," said the cook. "Perhaps I simply misplaced—"

But her more reasonable voice vanished under the escalating shouts of Mr. and Mrs. Sullivan, both so belligerent that Jon couldn't even make out what they were individually saying—just snatches like "insult our guest!" and "invite that element into our home!" and "*our* home?"

And Grace—Grace looked stricken.

At that point, Jon didn't care whether anybody thought he was being forward or not. He was getting Grace out of there. "Come on," he shouted into her ear, and pulled her chair out with one hand before he managed to lever himself to his good foot. "We should probably leave them alone."

Grace nodded, her china blue eyes immediately grateful, and when Jon opened his hand to her, she put her smaller hand in it. He drew her to her feet—and wished he didn't have to let go of her to get his crutches.

But maybe it was just as well. Belle and Charisma had circled the table to lead their younger sister out.

Jon followed on his crutches, in short swings, waiting until Comtesse Arabella had swept stiffly by him to shut the door.

Something smashed against the dining room wall, from inside, and for a long moment nobody said anything.

So Jon whistled low and said, "I've been in barroom brawls less raucous than that."

Charisma giggled then, high-pitched and nervous. Belle raised an eyebrow—he guessed that hadn't been the best comment to make.

Grace stood there, her arms wrapped about her front, and looked ill.

Comtesse Arabella said, "Well, really!" and swept away to the stairs in a stiff rustle of petticoats and another wafting of floral scent. *Good riddance.*

"I really didn't steal anything," Jon added quickly, in case anybody—in case Grace—honestly thought that. "You're welcome to send someone up to search—"

Which was when he had a pair of sickening thoughts. The first was that he shouldn't invite anybody to search his rooms, because they would probably find the stowaway.

The second was that, for all he knew about that stowaway, they might also find the silver. If he weren't using crutches, he might have wrapped his arms around *his* middle at the feeling that evoked in him.

Luckily, Belle said, "I'm sure that will not be necessary, Mr. Erikson. Mother is just . . . um . . . sensitive about some matters."

". . . *you pig-headed, low-class, stone-blind son of a . . .*" screamed her sensitive mother, in the next room. Jon cleared his throat noisily over the last word of her insult, just in case it was what he thought it would be.

Charisma looked intrigued.

Grace still looked sick, and who could blame her?

The hell with propriety. Jon put a steadying hand on Grace's shoulder and winced down at her. "Are you all right?"

She met his gaze with desperation, and at that moment he wanted nothing more than to grab her, grab the kid, and get them all out of this madhouse.

To where? It was a stupid idea, and he knew it. It was also the opposite of everything he'd worked toward. *To what?*

This really was a madhouse, if he was starting to think like that.

"If that boy goes," bellowed Patrick Sullivan, somewhat muffled beyond the door, *"I'm going with him!"*

And his wife screamed, "Don't be letting the door hit you on the—"

"Look at her," Jon said to Belle, effectively distracting the oldest daughter's horrified fascination away from the argument and back to her sister. "She shouldn't be listening to this."

"He's never threatened to leave before," said Grace softly, lifting round eyes to meet their concern. "Never once."

"Mr. Erikson's right, Grace," said Belle, scooping her sister toward her—and out from under Jon's comforting hand—then drawing her toward the stairs. "It doesn't do any good to listen to them."

"Papa threatens all sorts of things," added Charisma, draping her arm around Grace from the other side. "You know as well as we do that when he shouts something he hardly ever goes through with it. It's the things he says quietly we have to watch out for."

Grace, letting herself be led off, said, "But we wouldn't hear it if he said it quietly."

"Come on," insisted Charisma. "Let's go to Belle's room and figure out what has happened to the missing silver, so that Mama won't fret about it anymore."

Jon watched them go, his frustration hardening into anger. He was angry with Mrs. Sullivan for believing he'd sink to thievery, and with Mr. Sullivan for effectively hobbling him—if Jon left, then so would Patrick? Patrick had a family to take care of! He was angry with both Sullivans for shouting in front of their daughters like that. He was angry at the very idea that Gio might be their silver thief. He was angry with himself for caring so much, after barely a week in Colorado Springs, and for breaking his leg and stranding himself here in the first place. And he was angry with Grace for . . .

No. He'd told her she wasn't at fault for falling on him, and she wasn't. He wouldn't let her be. He'd be glad to have caught her if he'd broken both legs and an arm.

But it didn't stop him from being angry. And more or less helpless—except for one point. It was enough to get him tackling the stairs, and glad for the exertion.

He could at least make sure he hadn't been feeding cookies to a little silver thief.

Chapter Eight

By the time Grace and her sisters reached Belle's bedroom, Grace felt embarrassed to have required such coddling. She might be the youngest, but she wasn't a baby. She was eighteen, for mercy's sake! Some of her friends were already married, already mothers, at eighteen. Surely she could handle a simple family argument.

Except that the more often her parents fought, the sicker she felt about it. And now Da's threat to leave . . .

She could think of little worse than not to have her family together. And with Belle and Charisma already engaged to be married . . .

What would she do if the whole family disintegrated?

She felt embarrassed to require special attention, and yet infinitely grateful to her sisters, and to Jon, for providing it. Especially Jon. When the shouting began, she'd felt as if she were caught in some kind of whirlpool. When Jon gave her his hand to help her up, everything had gone steady again.

She wished that instead of coming to Belle's room, she'd gone up to his. But that was a very un-ladylike wish.

"It wasn't always this bad, was it?" she asked her sisters. She sat carefully in a chair while Charisma firmly shut the door. Now she had to strain her ears to hear even the loudest of shouts. She couldn't make out words anymore. Maybe that was a good thing. "The way they fight. It was never like this when we were little, was it?"

"No," said Belle, sinking onto her bed. "It wasn't this bad before, Gracie. It's getting worse."

"Which doesn't make sense." Charisma chose pacing over sitting. "We've spent half a year giving Mother reasons to be happy, so that she won't feel she must try so hard!"

"Is that what we've been doing?" challenged Belle, lifting an eyebrow.

"Perhaps it was not our immediate goal," admitted Charisma. "But that was part of it. In fact, when we drove out to the Garden of the Gods last spring, didn't Mama *tell* us to wish for husbands?"

They all remembered the picnic to which Charisma referred—the one that had changed the lives of the two older Sullivan girls, if not Grace's. Not yet, anyway.

"'Men of breeding and substance,'" quoted Belle. "That's what Mama wanted for us."

Exactly the kind of man Jon wasn't. "But we didn't," said Grace, hesitant. "That's what Mama *wanted* us to wish for, but we didn't do that."

Instead, stinging at their escorts' mockery of them, they'd wished for beauty, charm, and grace.

"And we've gotten both," Charisma reminded her. "Belle is prettier and engaged to Kit Stanhope. I've learned to mind my tongue—sometimes—and I've found Will. You'd think Mama would be ecstatic."

"Except I haven't gotten either one." Grace fidgeted with one of the blue silk flowers on her dress. She could wear a corset and bustle, but she was still dangerous at a dinner table. If Jon hadn't caught that glob of pudding, it would have hit Da square in the face.

She still wasn't sure which would have been worse.

She said, "Even after a week with Comtesse Arabella, I'm not a bit more elegant, and I haven't found a man of breeding and substance, either. Maybe that's why Mama's still not happy."

"Don't you dare think that, Grace Sullivan," warned Belle. "This is not your fault."

"But you've both said that once we're all three spoken for, Mama won't feel she must try so hard. And once Da sees that we're happy, he won't be as angry with her."

"In fact," said Charisma, "little though we might want to admit it, some of Belle's and my happiness is directly due to Mama's machinations. I wish Papa realized that."

"She *is* the one who paid Kit to step out with me that first time," admitted Belle with a blush. "And she's hired the *comtesse* to help Grace."

Grace wished she could feel more grateful about that. "And she wants me to encourage Robert James's attentions. Do you . . . do you think she might be right about that, too?"

She didn't think so, herself. While not an unpleasant man, Robert James was just . . . there. But she was having a hard time thinking clearly around thoughts of summertime blue eyes.

"It's not as if you're being pursued by anyone

else," said Charisma. "So what could it hurt? We just want you to be as happy as we are, Grace."

"Exactly," said Belle. "And if you don't get to know him, how will you ever know for sure?"

Downstairs, something else crashed loudly enough to be heard through two closed doors.

"No," said Grace softly. "How will I ever know?"

And how could she possibly make everyone happy?

"If you tell me you've been stealing silver," announced Jon to his empty bedroom as he swung in, "I will wring your skinny little neck."

Then, since the gaslight was already lit, he shut his bedroom door behind him. As soon as the latch clicked, Gio crawled out from under the bed, eyes wide as ever. "You would really wring my neck?"

"Or maybe just . . . just beat you until you couldn't sit down." Jon put down his crutches and deliberately fell, face first, across his bed, squashing his nose against the coverlet. He knew he couldn't beat the kid, either. Not even if Gio were *his* kid. And he wasn't.

He turned his head to see the boy again. "Or send you to an orphanage," he warned. "You *aren't* stealing silver, are you?"

Gio shook his head vehemently, then crawled onto the bed beside Jon and lay down with his arms at his side, mimicking the larger man's position, so they were almost nose to nose. "They are yelling about silver?"

"They're yelling about *missing* silver," agreed Jon, then considered it. "Among other things."

"From the mines?"

"From the kitchen."

"Oh." Gio said nothing else until Jon rolled onto his shoulder to see the kid without straining his neck quite so badly. Gio rolled onto his shoulder, too, and asked, "Who do they think took it?"

"At least one of them thinks I did." Jon was a good-natured fellow. He hadn't felt this angry in a long time. "That's one too many."

"They are fools!" protested Gio.

Jon ruffled the boy's hair, touched. "Thank you."

"Will—will you leave here, then?" Clearly, the kid didn't want him to. But Jon *had* to leave, sooner or later—and the sooner, the better. He was a prospector, after all. Fortune's companion. Destiny's beau. He'd wanted this adventure forever, and his father's illness had lingered, and lingered. . . . Not that Jon wouldn't give up all hope of adventure for more time with his father. But it was over, and his only consolation was, now he was finally supposed to be free.

Free of responsibility. Free of small-town limitations. Free to make his *own* way at last, instead of being defined by his family. But as long as he was stuck here . . .

"I can't leave yet," he admitted. "Not until I'm sure Sullivan won't move out in protest. He's got a family to take care of."

It shouldn't matter to him who stayed and who went. It shouldn't matter to him if Grace Sullivan's family life was a mess. Other people's happiness was none of his doing.

Which was why it unnerved him when Gio lit up

in smiles at the news that Jon wasn't leaving yet. "Good!"

"Not good," Jon protested. "Mrs. Sullivan thinks I'm a thief."

"But you are *not* a thief," Gio reminded him with the simplicity of youth. Then he blinked, looking cynical—and mischievous—again. "Are you?"

Jon couldn't help it—he grinned. "Watch it, kid."

"Because I should have to wring your—" The rest Gio lost in giggles, because Jon was tickling him. When the kid could no longer breathe for hiccuping, Jon lifted him up high over his head.

"P—put me down!" It came out, "Putta me down!"

"Not until you say . . ." Hmm, what to make him say? "Not until you say, 'Jon is always right.'"

"No!"

So Jon used his good leg to stand momentarily and thus drop the child into the middle of the down mattress from the highest possible height. Then—unable to stand for long anyway—he fell on him for more tickles. But Gio was a squirmy kid; he managed to get some pretty good tickles in himself.

It was a good thing the Sullivans were fighting so loudly downstairs, as much noise as Jon and the kid were making.

"Hey!" Jon protested with a laugh as Gio got in a good swipe at his ribs. "No fair."

"Yes, fair!" But once Jon lifted Gio high over his head again, the little boy's dark eyes sparkling and his black curls hanging downward, Gio said, "*This* is not fair."

"Of course it is, because I'm always right."

Gio kicked his bare feet in midair.

"Say it," Jon warned, heaving himself up onto his

good leg again. He braced the knee of his cast leg against the bed for balance.

Gio shook his head, almost hitting the ceiling, and giggled.

"*Who's* always right?" challenged Jon.

"I am!"

So Jon tossed him into the mattress. When Gio clambered out of the downy softness to lunge at him, Jon caught him with a hand on top of his head and held him at arm's reach while the kid squirmed. "*I'm* always right, aren't I? Say—"

Someone knocked on the door.

Jon spun, then lost his balance and sat hard on the bed. He heard a soft thud behind him as Gio dived for the floor. "Uh—come in?"

The door opened, and the cook—Phronsy—smiled at where Jon sat too stiffly, his good shirt half pulled out of his pants, on a very messy bed. Then she turned and vanished from the doorway.

"You okay?" whispered Jon, afraid to turn around.

"Uh-huh," whispered Gio.

In a moment the cook was back, carrying a tray. "Dinner ended rather abruptly," she explained. "I thought perhaps you would enjoy a snack."

She set the tray on the bedside table, smiled, and left, closing the door firmly behind her.

It took several heartbeats before Jon could even start breathing again. That had been too close!

Gio cautiously circled the bed, crawling. "Did she hear?"

"She had to." They'd sometimes heard footsteps through that door. How could someone not hear a squealing eight-year-old?

"Maybe she's deaf." Gio sat up to lift the corner of a napkin from the basket it covered. He grinned to discover doughnut twists. "She's old."

"She's not that old." Jon reached past the kid to help himself. The pastry was still warm. When he took a bite, it was delicious, too.

But it was also just a treat. He frowned. "And you should have more than doughnuts for dinner."

"I did," protested Gio, clearly proud. "While you were eating, I snuck downstairs and made a sandwich, with pot roast and carrots and bread. It was a very good sandwich."

It occurred to Jon that Gio's sandwich counted as theft. The food he got off Jon's trays was one thing, but helping himself in the kitchen . . .

Then again, the Sullivans could afford it. Should the child go hungry?

Maybe some moral issues weren't so clear-cut after all.

"I guess that's okay, then." He retrieved one of the two tankards of milk from the tray. "At least drink this."

Then he froze, looking at his hand.

He looked at the tray. There sat a second tankard of milk.

He looked at Gio, who, though a quarter his size, caught on faster. "Uh-oh," said the kid, then tried Jon's version. "*Uff da?*"

Phronsy knew.

Grace woke before dawn, as she usually did, and crawled out from under her purring, cat-draped quilt. She washed and dressed as quickly as possible, glad for the radiator heat. She and her sisters could think of nobody who might be stealing the silver—not Jon, not Comtesse Arabella, and not the maid or the cook. So they'd decided, during their discussion the night before, to ask Phronsy for more details.

Grace had happily volunteered. After all, she woke earliest of all of them. And she very much hoped Phronsy would let her help make breakfast.

She didn't feel anywhere near as incompetent in the kitchen as she did in the ballroom.

"I only noticed it missing a few days ago," said Phronsy, moving effortlessly from the big sink with its indoor pump to the even larger cast-iron stove, to the wooden table where Grace sat, stirring pancake batter. Phronsy had let her measure in every bit of the ingredients and hadn't even minded the flour and water now making a paste on the floor. "It may have vanished earlier, but I think it started when the guests arrived and we began carrying all those trays back and forth."

Like Jon, Comtesse Arabella had been taking her breakfast on a tray, though not because she was in any way impaired—she simply liked breakfast in bed, and much later than everyone else. But she was noble; why would *she* steal spoons?

"The missing spoons are the ones you used on the trays?" asked Grace, accidentally slopping some of the batter out of the bowl and into her aproned lap. "Oh . . ."

Uff da.

Phronsy made a detour from her usual choreography to scoop her hands under Grace's apron, lift the pool of batter up, and scrape it off the linen and back into the bowl. "The apron's clean," said the cook simply, and went back to work.

Grace smiled, relieved by the lack of waste, and continued stirring.

"I cannot say the very spoons that are missing were on the trays," said Phronsy, sprinkling water droplets off her fingertips onto the stove. "But the missing pieces are the pattern that we used on the trays."

Grace considered it, then asked a question that worried her. "Do you suppose *I* could have lost them, dropped them maybe, and not known it?"

"Not likely," said Phronsy. "Silverware tends to fall loudly. More likely that when I collected the trays, I simply did not notice spoons. Or the lack."

Which brought them back to Jon and the *comtesse*. Of the two, Grace knew whom she would rather suspect.

The one who was not polite to people outside her social circle—that was who!

The one without summertime blue eyes.

"I did not immediately mention it to your mother," said Phronsy, "because I was certain that they would turn up. I am still certain of this. There. The griddle is hot enough; bring the batter."

Grace stared at her, eyes widening. "You want *me* . . . ?"

"Yes. See?" When Phronsy sprinkled more water on the flat griddle, the droplets danced and sizzled across its surface. "Be careful, though. It is hot."

Grace looked at the stove—huge, and black, and nickel-trimmed. It was far larger than her, and Phronsy was right—it was hot.

The pancake batter smelled so good in her mixing bowl.

With a deep breath, she stood and stepped carefully forward.

The stove did nothing to stop her.

She used her mixing spoon to lift a pool of batter from the bowl, moved it carefully over the griddle—and the spoon somehow slipped from her hand. *Splash!*

"Oh! I'm sorry," said Grace quickly. Some mornings she wondered if those had been her first words in life. "I'm *so* sorry."

"Stoves wash," said Phronsy easily, recovering the spoon and handing it back to Grace. Then she smiled. "Look. You made a star."

And sure enough, the splat of batter on the griddle had formed a star shape. Of sorts.

Grace felt some of the tension down her spine ease. "Then, it doesn't matter that it's not round? I'm . . . I'm truly not very graceful, you know."

"That depends on what you mean by 'graceful,'" said Phronsy mysteriously. "And griddle cakes taste as good, no matter the shape. Try again."

So Grace made pancakes. Some of them came out as very strange shapes, although she and Phronsy had as much fun naming them as Grace once had trying to see shapes in the clouds. Some of the pancakes ended up as near-perfect circles. Batter, she learned, was very forgiving when making circles.

A few of them, just for fun, she deliberately poured into other shapes: half-moons, and rings, and bows. But then it occurred to her that her mother and Comtesse Arabella probably wanted simple, unimaginative, round pancakes.

"That is all right," said Phronsy. "I know someone who would very much like a moon shape."

"Who?" asked Grace.

But the doorway from the servants' stairs opened, and Jon Erikson sidled through, braced on his crutches. He looked good and fresh this morning, in his usual dungarees and chambray shirt and suspenders. His hair was slightly damp, several buttons of his collar unbuttoned. And his eyes widened when he caught sight of her by the stove.

Grace stared right back, forgetting that she had a spoonful of batter in her hand. She heard a gentle sizzle.

Phronsy looked over her shoulder and nodded at whatever shape she'd just poured. "Lighting bolt," she decided.

The first thing Jon did, he had to admit, was stare. That was Grace? She stood beside the stove as if she belonged there, her apron stained, flour whitening the end of her nose, and she looked . . . happy.

Until now, he hadn't seen her happy very often. Even in his room, talking with him, she'd tempered her pleasure with wariness of getting caught.

The second thing Jon did, almost too late to matter, was to shove his hand back through the door to the servants' stairs and gesture Gio back before the little boy could come in and give himself away.

"Grace!" said Jon, loudly enough that Gio could hear.

The door slowly shut behind him. So much for

his idea of confronting Phronsy to learn how much she knew about Gio. Jon had been nearly asleep last night when it had come to him: the perfect solution! If Phronsy knew about Gio, maybe had known about him since he followed her to the Sullivan household, then she might be willing to take responsibility for the kid when Jon left. Gio would be warm, and safe, and—heaven knew—well fed. And Jon would be free to keep company with Fortune and Destiny.

Not that he mentioned that part of the plan to Gio, both because he wasn't sure how the cook would take to it, and because he suspected the kid would prefer heading into the mountains in search of gold. All Jon had said was that they should thank Phronsy for the doughnuts, milk, and silence. Gio, thrilled to leave the room with him for once, had readily agreed, and showed him the private back stairs.

But now Grace was here. Distraction or not, delay or not, it was still a good thing.

"Jon," she said, looking equally surprised, then put her mixing spoon in the large bowl she held and put the bowl carefully on the table behind her. "I mean, Mr. Erikson."

"I didn't know you cooked," he said. Then he sniffed the air, redolent with scents of sweetness and meat and butter. "It smells wonderful."

"Most of that's Phronsy," Grace said quickly. "She's just letting me help."

"Miss Grace is modest," said Phronsy, cracking eggs into a skillet. "She made the griddle cakes alone."

"I love griddle cakes," said Jon. As if to punctuate

the idea, his stomach growled. He grinned, cha-
grined.

Grace smiled back. "I'll get you some."

"Oh! Uh . . ." Bad enough to be downstairs eating while Gio was upstairs and hungry . . . or forced
to raid the kitchen. But to eat practically in front of
the kid . . .

"Do sit down," insisted Phronsy, indicating a
chair opposite the stairway door. "I have some griddle cakes that are perhaps a little too dark; I shall
put them in the pantry for the cats."

Was she saying what Jon thought she was saying?
He swung over to the chair and sat. Grace was too
busy fixing his plate—not just with griddle cakes
but bacon and eggs and muffins—to notice that
Phronsy was setting the "cats" up with butter and
molasses. Then, as Grace had her back to the door,
setting Jon's plate so carefully in front of him that
she looked to be holding her breath, Phronsy simply opened the door from the stairs and waved the
little boy—grinning widely—across the corner of
the kitchen and through the door to the pantry.

She passed the plate in after him and left that
door cracked.

A little hand poked out of the crack and waved.

Jon had a sinking feeling this wasn't going to last
long. Then he looked up at Grace and didn't care
so much. She sure was pretty at this time of morning.

"My mother always told me it's rude to eat in
front of a lady unless she eats, too," he warned, and
Grace hesitated.

"Go ahead," urged Phronsy, bringing another
plate to the table. "Just a little."

So Grace sat across from him—and stared, looking from him to his plate to him. Finally, she asked, "Isn't it good?"

"I'll tell you as soon as you try a bite," Jon prompted. When she looked confused, he said, "My mother always told me . . ."

"Oh!" And she took a quick bite of pancakes.

Relieved, Jon dug in. He really was hungry. "These are delicious," he said, chewing, and they were.

Instead of protesting his poor table manners, Grace beamed. "Thank you. It's Phronsy's recipe."

"And Grace's personal touch," added Phronsy.

"I accidentally dropped in a whole piece of cinnamon." Grace blushed. "We couldn't fish it all out."

"We fished out exactly enough," said Phronsy from the stove.

"The two of you," said Jon, cutting another piece and sliding it through a puddle of molasses, "make a great team. It's very good."

Then he shut up to simply eat. He noticed Phronsy bringing a tankard of milk to the pantry and grinned his thanks at her. Then he noticed Grace staring at him.

Her elbow propped on the table. Her chin propped on her fist. Staring.

She seemed to like what she saw.

Jon's chewing slowed. "What?"

"You eat as if you like it," said Grace, watching his eyes.

He blinked. The food wasn't the only thing he liked. "I do," he said. "I said so."

She nodded happily.

He wasn't sure what to say to that, so he went back to eating. A few minutes later, Grace stood and went back to pouring pancake batter on the griddle.

Good food. Ladies making it. Snow outside, and the redolent warmth of the kitchen inside. It didn't get a lot better than this, did it?

Except, thought Jon, that he wanted to be prospecting. Or at least holed up with other miners—working miners, not mine owners—waiting for spring. He wasn't the shopkeeping type. He didn't plan to do ranch work or railroad work. He didn't have the education to do the kind of work Will Barclay did, or the family background to live like Kit Stanhope. All he wanted was to meet Mother Nature on her own terms and coax her to give up a little of her treasure.

And that meant not getting used to mornings like this.

Still, it was hard to do while he sat here, enjoying the best griddle cakes he'd ever eaten and watching Grace at the stove. He noticed the gentle fall of her skirt from her waist to the floor, and how her apron strings trailed into its pleats. He noticed how her bodice plumped out over her bosom as she hugged the mixing bowl to her. He noticed how she bit her lower lip.

Jon slowly became aware of a completely different hunger. He wanted to free that lip from between her teeth and kiss it to make it better. He wanted to nuzzle the flour off Grace's cheek, her nose. And then, while he had her in his arms . . .

He cleared his throat and took another bite of

pancakes. This was not why he'd come down to the kitchen. And yet . . .

"Miss Grace, how old are you?" he asked.

She startled from her reverie of watching him, spilling some pancake batter onto the griddle. Glancing quickly down at her damage, she softly said, "Cat." Then she told him, "I'm eighteen. I just turned eighteen this January."

He'd thought she was younger. Things would be much simpler if she were younger.

"Why do you ask?" She cocked her head, considering him. "How old are *you*, Mr. Erikson?"

"I'm twenty-three," he said. "And I only asked because . . . well, because . . ."

Because I'm having the kind of thoughts about you that an honorable man wouldn't have about a much younger girl, that's why.

"My sisters learned to cook much younger than you," was what he said.

It clearly was not what she'd wanted to hear. "Oh." She turned back to her batter. "Well, Mother taught us a little before we moved to Colorado Springs. But I was only eleven then, when Da got rich, and the house was built. And after that, Mama said that real ladies let the hired help do the cooking."

Jon sighed. "She would."

Which was when Grace surprised him. She stood up straighter. Her eyes flashed at him. She slopped a spoonful of batter onto the griddle without even looking to see what shape it made. And she demanded, "What's that supposed to mean?"

Chapter Nine

For the first time since he'd met her, Grace Sullivan showed signs of a temper—and it was aimed at him?

"I'll have you know that my mother is a fine woman!" she announced, firmly dishing out more spoonsful of batter: one, two, three. "She's been trying very hard, harder than you can imagine, to make ladies out of all of us—herself included—and it's not easy for her. She used to work as a domestic herself, when she was younger than me. Once she married Da, she baked for the miners to get us through the winters. She doesn't want us to have to do the same, that's all. Is that so bad?"

Jon said, "That depends on who she hurts in the name of refinement."

"She did not actually accuse you of anything," Grace pointed out, though at least she had the decency to look less sure on that point. "She looked at you when she learned of the silver, which was silly since of course you didn't steal it, but that's not the same as accusing you."

She flipped the pancakes then, in angry, easy turns. One, two, three.

Something about that niggled at Jon's attention,

but he was too busy admiring what Grace Sullivan became when she got her Irish up. Surely that flush in her cheeks, that sparkle in her eyes, was from more than the stove!

"I wasn't," said Jon, "talking about me."

"Well, who else is she possibly hurting?"

"You!"

Grace's mouth fell open in pure shock. Then she shut it, shook her head, and scooped the done pancakes off the griddle onto the plate by the stove. "My mother wouldn't hurt me."

"Not on purpose." Jon felt rather bad for mentioning it, now. It being the truth eased some of his worst guilt, though.

"Not at all! Why, Jon . . . I mean, Mr. Erikson . . ."

Jon folded his arms. "I think Phronsy's figured out that you call me Jon." He could only hope that Phronsy wasn't a gossip, or his hours in this house were likely numbered. Considering her help with Gio, he was probably still stuck here.

Grace ladled more batter onto the griddle, her movements smooth and natural—and Jon realized what it was that had caught his attention. *Interesting.* She said, "How can you say my mother's hurting me in the name of refinement? The refinement is *for* me."

"That's what she's telling you, but it's a pile of manure," Jon insisted. "You don't need refinement."

"Of course I do!"

How could she be so blind? "Well, I think you're wonderful just the way you are!"

The words slipped out before he could stop them, and just hung there in the warm kitchen air between them.

Take A Trip Into A Timeless World of Passion and Adventure with Kensington Choice Historical Romances!
—Absolutely FREE!

Enjoy the passion and adventure of another time with Kensington Choice Historical Romances. They are the finest novels of their kind, written by today's best-selling romance authors. Each Kensington Choice Historical Romance transports you to distant lands in a bygone age. Experience the adventure and share the delight as proud men and spirited women discover the wonder and passion of true love.

Get 4 FREE Books!

We created our convenient Home Subscription Service so you'll be sure to have the hottest new romances delivered each month right to your doorstep—usually before they are available in book stores. Just to show you how convenient the Zebra Home Subscription Service is, we would like to send you 4 FREE Kensington Choice Historical Romances. The books are worth up to $24.96, but you only pay $1.99 for shipping and handling. There's no obligation to buy additional books—ever!

Save Up To 30% With Home Delivery!

Accept your FREE books and each month we'll deliver 4 brand new titles as soon as they are published. They'll be yours to examine FREE for 10 days. Then if you decide to keep the books, you'll pay the preferred subscriber's price (up to 30% off the cover price!), plus shipping and handling. Remember, you are under no obligation to buy any of these books at any time! If you are not delighted with them, simply return them and owe nothing. But if you enjoy Kensington Choice Historical Romances as much as we think you will, pay the special preferred subscriber rate and save over $8.00 off the cover price!

we have 4 FREE BOOKS for you as your
introduction to
KENSINGTON CHOICE!
To get your FREE BOOKS, worth up to $24.96, mail
the card below or call TOLL-FREE 1-800-770-1963.
Visit our website at www.kensingtonbooks.com.

Get 4 FREE Kensington Choice Historical Romances!

♡ **YES!** Please send me my 4 FREE KENSINGTON CHOICE HISTORICAL ROMANCES (without obligation to purchase other books). I only pay $1.99 for shipping and handling. Unless you hear from me after I receive my 4 FREE BOOKS, you may send me 4 new novels—as they are published—to preview each month FREE for 10 days. If I am not satisfied, I may return them and owe nothing. Otherwise, I will pay the money-saving preferred subscriber's price (over $8.00 off the cover price), plus shipping and handling. I may return any shipment within 10 days and owe nothing, and I may cancel any time I wish. In any case the 4 FREE books will be mine to keep.

Name _____

Address _____ Apt. _____

City _____ State _____ Zip _____

Telephone (____) _____

Signature _____

(If under 18, parent or guardian must sign)

Offer limited to one per household and not to current subscribers. Terms, offer and prices subject to change. Orders subject to acceptance by Kensington Choice Book Club.
Offer Valid in the U.S. only.

KN014A

KENSINGTON CHOICE

Zebra Home Subscription Service, Inc.

P.O. Box 5214

Clifton NJ 07015-5214

Grace blinked at him . . . and belatedly put down her bowl of batter. "You do?"

Jon had the strongest urge to run. To run far and fast. But when he pushed back his chair, a twinge in his hurt leg reminded him of the problems there. So instead he just stood and collected his crutches from the wall.

He felt better knowing he could at least limp away. "Yes," he admitted. "I do. If I weren't heading out as soon as my leg heals, Grace, I might even do something about that. But you're doing everything you can to become some kind of highfalutin' lady, and I'm just a prospector—"

"Do what?" asked Grace, crossing the kitchen to stand in front of him. She looked vaguely stunned. It was a cute look on her, especially with the flour on her nose . . . but weren't they all cute looks? "What might you do about it?"

Run. But Jon was on crutches. He couldn't run. So he kissed her, right there in the kitchen.

He hadn't thought it out—thinking was never his strong suit, and around Grace he felt even more impaired. He just knew that his fingers ached to feel her hair, so he braced his weight on one crutch, one leg, and slid his freed hand into her coppery curls. He just knew that his lips hungered for hers far more than he had for pancakes, so he bent over, and with a soft brush of mouth on mouth, he tasted her. So soft. So innocent.

When he straightened from the kiss, Grace just stared up at him, eyes wide, her lips parted. Jon shifted uncomfortably. Was she angry? Was she glad?

He heard a noise from the pantry, and on the

edge of his vision he noticed another face with big dark eyes and an open mouth. Now they had an audience.

He also noticed Grace starting to turn that way. So he quickly kissed her again for distraction.

Grace hadn't recovered from the first kiss before Jon ducked his head to hers and covered her mouth with his own a second time. And oh, she liked it! He almost had to curl around her to bend that far; between that and his fingers gently supporting her head, she felt protected and special. His lips were as soft as she'd hoped, and they tasted like molasses and cinnamon, and Grace felt the strangest sensation of satisfaction and yet of dizziness. . . .

Her knees simply went out from under her, and she dropped.

Jon caught her around the waist, drew her against him as a crutch clattered to the floor. "Gracie? Miss Sullivan, are you all right? I'm so sorry—I—"

The second crutch fell, and he sort of hobbled her back to the table, to the chair he'd been sitting in, and laid her into it, sinking onto his knees beside her. "Did *I* do that? I am so—"

But she draped her arms over his shoulders and closed her eyes and kissed him a third time, effectively silencing him.

She could feel his lips turn up into a smile against her own. Then Jon's strong arms came around her, and he was holding her close against him and enthusiastically kissing her, his lips still moving but not just to smile, his nose nuzzling beside her nose. Grace stretched into the languid sensation of it the way she might stretch into sunshine after a long winter. He thought she was *wonderful!*

Nearby, a throat cleared.

Grace opened her eyes slowly to the heavy-lidded, blue-eyed beauty of her miner friend—more than a friend! No wonder Belle and Charisma liked kissing so well. Just being held would be sheer joy, but throw in the kissing, and she doubted she'd ever been so happy.

Again the throat cleared. Then Phronsy said, "Mr. Erikson, you are a guest in this house. And Grace Sullivan . . . your mother's kitchen!"

To Grace's great disappointment, Jon drew back from her. Only a few inches at first, but it was a few inches too many, to her way of thinking. "Uh . . . yeah," he murmured, his voice rich as crumbling pastry.

Grace thought, *My mother hardly even comes in here.*

But Phronsy hadn't been warning them; she'd been chiding them. And maybe she should.

From the way Jon was drawing farther back, fumbling for one of his crutches, he understood. "I, uh . . . Miss Grace, I shouldn't have done that."

And now that he wasn't holding her, wasn't kissing her, she knew that. She'd never completely understood what her sisters were talking about regarding invisible lines that one's beau shouldn't cross, but now that she'd crossed one, she knew it. For one thing, Jon would never make a proper beau for her. For another, he was leaving soon. He'd said so himself.

But she'd never enjoyed misbehaving more in

her whole life. Shouldn't have done it? "I suppose not," was all she managed.

"Can you ever forgive me?" He'd found his crutches and was standing, wincing at her.

Grace licked a trace of molasses off her lips and wondered why her knees still wouldn't work. "Oh, *yes*," she said fervently, her gaze clinging to his. "I forgive you."

His gaze went slightly unfocused at that, and he smiled a wonderful, goofy smile. "You do?"

Do it again, and I'll forgive you again. She blushed even to imagine saying something like that.

Jon's smile widened . . .

Then Phronsy stepped between them. "Perhaps you should go back upstairs, Mr. Erikson," said the cook sternly. "I will send *that other package* up to you later."

Package? Grace hardly cared. She touched her lips, remembering the kisses instead.

"Later," agreed Jon vaguely—then blinked and looked at the cook. "That other package. From the pantry, you mean."

"Yes," said Phronsy firmly. "From the pantry."

"That. Yeah, I'll want that. . . ." Jon tried to back up, but between his crutches and the paste on the floor, he stumbled, nearly fell, barely caught himself. He chuckled. "See? You're not the only person who can be a bit clumsy now and then. . . ."

Grace shook her head, happy. She wasn't, was she?

"In fact," said Jon, awkwardly reaching the back stairs, "you should cook more often, Grace. It's good for you."

"What do you mean?"

He held her gaze for a long moment—perhaps just because he liked holding her gaze. When he blinked back to thinking, it looked painful. "Look at those last batches of pancakes you made," he told her.

Then he turned, and he began the slow process of hopping up the stairs, helped only by the crutches.

There was no banister on the servants' staircase.

Once the door shut behind him, Grace felt she could begin to breathe again. Perhaps she hadn't been breathing. Perhaps that was why kissing him had made her so wonderfully dizzy. Dizzier than spinning around in the grass or rolling down a high, flowery hill.

"I didn't quite expect that," murmured Phronsy.

"What?" asked Grace, looking down at the floor. Jon had knelt on that floor, to better kiss her. She looked at her hands. During the third kiss, she'd curled her hands into his bronzed hair, which had been as soft as his lips, and thick, and wonderful. "What didn't you expect?"

Whatever it was, Phronsy shook her head to dismiss it. "Nothing, Miss Grace. That is . . . of course I did not expect such behavior in my kitchen. I could be fired if your parents learned of it. You know that, don't you?"

Grace found that she could sit up, could stand after all. She should have known that. "I'm sorry, Phronsy! We won't do it again, I promise. Not in the kitchen, anyway."

Phronsy did not look particularly soothed by that promise. But instead of commenting, she said, "The boy was right about one thing, though."

When Grace came to her side, the cook pointed out the last nine pancakes she'd made—all of them perfectly round, with nary a splatter.

Grace could hardly believe it. *She'd* made those?

"When I argued with Jon, I wasn't clumsy!"

What had he done?

As soon as he got back up to his room, Jon started to pack.

That took about two minutes, even with the awkwardness of the crutches. He'd never had much with him in the first place. Then he swung to the window, opened it, and gulped cold mountain air. He needed a little companionship from Fortune and Destiny to get him out of here. Now that he was ambulatory, he could leave—he didn't have much money to pay for boarding elsewhere, and he wasn't sure where to go, but he could physically take the steps. He would leave Patrick Sullivan a note insisting that it was not Bridey Sullivan's fault. He would ask Phronsy to take care of Gio. He would get away from Grace before he found himself so deeply involved with her that his concern became its own claim.

When he heard the door open behind him, he spun guiltily from the open window. Patrick Sullivan was paying for the coal that was heating the house—and the cold mountain air, thanks to Jon. But it was just the kid, black eyes shining with interest.

"You kissed her!"

"I shouldn't have," said Jon.

"Why not? She kissed you back, yes?"

The memory distracted Jon. Yeah. She had. Even if he hadn't learned her real age, that last kiss would have proved Grace Sullivan to be more woman than girl.

Then he noticed how pleased Gio looked, and shook off that thought. "She shouldn't have, either."

"But you like each other." Gio swung onto the bed. "And neither of you is married. You can marry each other and mine for her papa, and if she got sick, you could afford a doctor."

The kid's father hadn't been able to afford a doctor for his wife. Jon saw where this was heading, and it made his chest ache, which annoyed him. "Listen, kid, it's been fun spending time with you, but I've got to go. I'll talk to the cook, and maybe—"

"Go?" Gio looked confused, as if he'd suddenly lost the ability to understand English. "But you cannot . . ."

Then he saw Jon's pack, and his mouth worked for a moment before he turned beseeching eyes back to Jon. "Without me?"

"Yes, without you. I'm not your father, and I don't intend to be. I need to be leaving now, before I do something with Grace Sullivan that I can't take back."

Gio's black curls swung with the vehemence of his protest. "No! You cannot go yet!"

"I've *got* to go yet. I'm afraid if I don't . . ."

Hell, he already felt awful for having been so forward—and for having enjoyed it so much. Imagine how he'd feel after another few weeks.

"But you like it here!"

"No, Gio. I don't. I like you, and I like Grace, and I like Mr. Sullivan and Phronsy. Grace's sisters seem nice enough. But I hate living in this hot, stuffy room in this fancy, stuffy house. I need to be out in the open, following adventure."

"But I can follow adventure, too!"

"It's too dangerous for a little boy."

Gio's lower lip began to protrude. "But not too dangerous for a cripple?"

Well, that was uncalled for. "I'm not a cripple! I'm just a little . . . awkward." He'd be even more awkward in snow and ice. But, damn it, if he stayed, he could find himself far more handicapped than that. Broken legs healed. Some things didn't—just look at the Sullivans' domestic life. "It doesn't matter what you say, kid. You're staying behind, and that's final."

"It is not final!" Gio even swung to the floor to face off with Jon on that point.

Jon, luckily, stood much taller. "It's final if I say it's final."

"I hate you!"

Jon had half expected that, though he hadn't expected how much it would bother him. He folded his arms. "I'm sorry to hear it."

"I hate you, and I hope you . . . I hope you drown in a snowdrift!" decided the little boy, backing toward the door. "I hope you never find anything more than rocks!" He opened the door, seemed to search for something worse he could say, and landed on "And I never wanted you for my papa anyway!"

Then he ran out.

Followed immediately by a crash.

* * *

After her success with the pancakes, Grace felt quite sure of herself, bringing coffee up to Jon's room by way of apology. She went straight up the stairs and got the tray from inside the dumbwaiter, without even bothering to open the bedroom door first.

Now, if only she could manage what she had to say to Jon as easily . . . She must pay more attention to her lessons in comportment. She mustn't risk her reputation spending so much time with him. Surely he would understand, even without her having to add how little faith she had that, if she spent too much more time in his presence, she would not gladly risk his presence further.

As she approached the room, she heard shouting. And it didn't sound like Jon.

Then the door swung open. "I never wanted you for my papa, anyway!" And something small barreled right into her stomach.

Oh, dear.

The tray flew in one direction; the coffee urn and mug sailed in the other. Everything landed with an assortment of crashes—along with her and the little boy who'd run her down.

Both of them sat up quickly. As startled as Grace felt, the little boy seemed more so, wide-eyed and miserable. He looked at her, then at the broken shards of urn and mug and spreading coffee . . .

And he burst into tears.

Grace didn't know who he was, and wasn't ready to entertain the suspicions that the child's words urged her toward. All she knew was that an adorable little boy was sitting in her family's third-floor hallway, crying.

She put her arms around him and drew him to her, not even bothering to stand first.

"Shhh," she said, patting his back. His hair made her think of a black lamb's—wild and curly—and his gulping sobs echoed something that had been wanting to get out of her for some time. "It's all right, little boy. I've smashed more pieces of crockery than you can probably count."

In fact, she remembered to call her usual "I've got it!" downstairs so nobody would come to investigate right off. She knew how *she* hated people staring at her clumsiness.

The little boy shook his head, as if to protest that the crockery wasn't the problem. Uncertain what was, Grace simply held him and rocked him.

She liked how his skinny little arms wrapped around her, and how his curly head burrowed into her shoulder. She felt oddly . . . needed.

Then Jon appeared in the doorway—and stared. "Oh, boy," he said, looking guilty.

That and the little boy's accusations were more than enough for Grace Sullivan. "You have a *son?*"

Bad enough to have kept such a thing secret from her, when she'd thought they were friends. But his secrecy implied something worse even than the possibility of his being a widower or, worse yet, having a wife. Something so scandalous that she ought not even know about its possibility. And to think, she'd kissed this man!

Jon's blue eyes narrowed. "No, I don't have a son."

The little boy turned his wet, reproachful face upward. "Papa, why do you say that?"

Jon Erikson said a bad word, and it wasn't *Uf da*. "The kid is lying, Grace."

The boy collapsed back into Grace's arms, sobbing a broken repeat of the word: "Papa . . ."

"Gio," warned Jon. *"Stop it."*

"So you do know him?" Grace kissed the top of the boy's head, tightening her hold.

"Yes, I know him; I just . . ." Jon bit back his words, glaring down the hall. "Look, Grace. Can we please discuss this in my room?"

"He keeps me hidden away," snuffled Gio. "Like his crazy aunt."

The monster!

Rather than look repentant, Jon folded his arms. "If Grace's parents find you, I'm not the one who's going to end up in an orphanage, now, am I?"

And like that, the boy's tears stopped. "Oh."

Maybe the child understood, but Grace certainly did not! "You would send your own son to an orphanage?"

Jon reached toward her, but it was to catch the little boy by the seat of his pants and physically lift him away from Grace. "He's not my son," he repeated, swinging the boy through the doorway. "But I've got to take some responsibility for him being here. If you'd just come in a moment . . ."

Now he held his big, warm hand out for her.

Grace wasn't sure what to do about this new turn of events. She'd meant to all but say good-bye to Jon, but surely she had to learn what was going on with little Gio first. She ought not be in his room, but he'd said something about the boy going to an orphanage if he were caught. Perhaps she should know more of their story before she risked that.

Besides, this was far more fascinating than lessons in comportment!

So she gave her hand to Jon and let him draw her up easily, then preceded him into the guest room.

Chapter Ten

Jon shut the door behind her, which he ought not to have done—even more interesting! The window sat open, so Grace went to stand by it. She liked breathing the mountain air.

"I should go immediately to my parents, Mr. Erikson," she said as primly as she possibly could—especially considering how she'd misbehaved with this man, not an hour ago! "But I will let you explain yourself first. Who is this little boy?"

The little boy in question, sitting on the bed, looked toward Jon. He had large, dark eyes and curly black hair. He was an amazingly cute little boy.

"His name is Gio," said Jon. "He's been living secretly in your house ever since your mother hired Phronsy. I'd never seen him until I came here."

Grace shook her head, not wanting to believe the worst of Phronsy. A man with a motherless child was bad enough. A woman with a fatherless child would be even more scandalous. Should her parents learn of it, Phronsy would be dismissed immediately.

It had happened before, with servants at the homes of Grace's friends. That was how she knew what little she did about such matters.

Still, she supposed she must ask. "Do you mean to say that Phronsy . . . ?"

"No, he's not hers," said Jon. "He's an orphan. He followed her from Denver."

Well, that was a relief. Grace didn't want to imagine what the kitchen would be like without Phronsy there. She looked at the boy. "You've really been hiding here for that long?"

Gio nodded, clearly proud of himself.

"And the only person who knew about you was Jon?"

"I think the cook, she knows too," admitted Gio. "But only since last night."

"Why did you say Jon was your papa?"

Now the boy flattened his mouth shut and looked down at his bare feet, scowling, saying nothing.

Oh, dear. Grace felt ill equipped to handle something as complicated as this. She turned to Jon again. "You kept him a secret all this last week?"

He ducked his head and shrugged. "The kid has a way about him. . . ."

Well, that she could see. "But we should tell my parents."

Gio sat quickly up. "No! They will make me an orphan!"

Bracing himself with one crutch, Jon reached across the bed and gently ruffled the boy's hair. "You *are* an orphan," he reminded the child.

Then he looked back to Grace. "You're right. That's exactly what I should have done. I know the right thing doesn't change just because of the consequences. But, Gracie . . ." He winced, seeming embarrassed. "I felt sorry for the kid. He doesn't want to go to an orphanage, and I figured it was just for a little while. . . ."

Gracie. Grace liked hearing the pet name from Jon's mouth. She liked watching his casual affection for this stray he'd picked up. Something about that warmed a spot inside her that had felt cold for too long—and not in a good, mountain-winter kind of way.

Jon squared his shoulders. "I'll tell them now. I owe you that much."

Oh, how she admired him!

Then he said, "I'm leaving anyway," and the swelling warmth deep inside her guttered.

"What?"

"He is going away," repeated Gio, all but spitting the words.

What?

"He is a coward, and he is afraid of kissing you again."

What?

Jon winced again, then cracked open his summertime eyes. "That's not quite true."

"It is!" insisted Gio. "You said—"

But Jon muffled him by covering the child's face with one large hand and gently pushing the boy back onto the bed. "This is between me and Grace, Gio. Go hide in a dumbwaiter or something."

"No!"

"Gio—"

"Will you stay, if I leave you alone with her? Will you take me with you?"

Jon looked toward Grace instead of at the little boy. She swallowed hard under the intensity of his gaze. "I thought we were friends, kid. Friends don't force other friends to do anything they don't want to do."

Like staying when they didn't want to stay, thought Grace miserably. Or . . .

Or like kissing someone if they didn't want to be kissed.

Perhaps they ought not to have kissed in the kitchen this morning. But neither of them had forced it on the other. He'd seemed to like it. She knew she did. She'd liked being held in his big, hard arms. She'd liked him thinking she was wonderful just the way she was. She'd wanted to be wanted like that, with an ache she'd kept hidden from herself for too long.

When Gio sulkily clambered off the bed and slipped out the door, leaving her alone in Jon's room, Grace could hardly breathe past an intense mixture of disappointment that Jon was leaving, of admiration that he so wanted to do the right thing . . . and of hope.

Hope that he might kiss her again.

Even if it had to be a kiss good-bye.

Little boys were a pain; that's all there was to it. Jon didn't really mind letting the Sullivans know that he'd been hiding a little intruder the whole time he'd been partaking of their hospitality. Hell, it might give Patrick justification not to follow through on his "If Erikson goes, I go" threat of the previous night.

But he couldn't have Grace thinking it was her fault.

The way she stared at him, he couldn't be sure what she was thinking. But it must not be that he hadn't enjoyed kissing her. It must not be that he didn't want to kiss her again.

"I'm sorry, Gracie," he said, using the bedposts to help himself hobble around the foot of the bed. The endearment slid out as naturally as it had before. He liked thinking of her as a Gracie, a young lady who made funny shapes with her flapjacks and who didn't protest open windows in the winter. He liked that a lot better than the epitome of Grace into which Comtesse Arabella was trying to change her. Trying to ruin her. "Gio didn't say it right. You're not the reason I'm leaving."

"Then . . ." She had to stop to catch her breath— was the mountain air too cold? "Then why are you? Your leg's still broken. Can't you let it heal awhile longer?"

The way she tipped her pretty face up toward him, beseeching, packed a lot more power than Gio's pleading.

Jon tried to remember that Destiny and Fortune were his girls, and he sank onto the bed to put himself more at her height. "I could stay longer," he admitted, but hurried on before her relief became too palpable. "But I shouldn't. For one thing, I'm not sure I like who I become here. All I do is sit around and be lazy; I was raised to do work, Grace, to keep busy. And I'm keeping secrets from my hosts, as if I have a better right to decide if Gio should go to an orphanage than your parents do. Hell, maybe I'm misjudging them. Maybe they'd take him in, give him the home he needs."

Grace shook her head. "I don't think so. Mama won't even let me have a dog. Or a squirrel. I found a baby squirrel last year, and as soon as it was old enough, Mama made me set it free. She said ladies only keep cats."

Jon really didn't like Grace's mama. But he did like the idea that Grace could set something free for its own good. "But don't you think the squirrel was happier with other squirrels?"

She nodded, reluctant.

"Well, that's kind of like me. I'm going to be happier in the mountains, where there isn't central heating and the food doesn't come on silver trays."

To his relief, Grace slowly nodded. "I understand," she said. "It's a very . . . stuffy house, isn't it?"

Uff da. "It's fine for a lady," Jon hurried to assure her. "It's fine for an heiress. Just not a poor dirt miner."

Dissatisfaction still clouded her pretty face. "So it's not that you don't want to kiss me?"

Oh, good Lord in heaven, no. She looked so warm, and so curvy, and so caring . . .

"I *shouldn't* want to kiss you, Grace," Jon admitted. "Not with you being an heiress and all. Not with everything your father's done for me. But I've got to admit, there's nothing I want to do more."

The smile that lit Grace Sullivan's face only increased the temptation. She ducked her head, suddenly shy of her own pleasure, but peeked back at him. "Nobody's ever wanted to kiss me before," she admitted.

"That's got to be a lie."

"Really! I think they're scared of me."

That was too much for Jon to take. He stood on his good foot and held his hands out for Grace, and drew her to him. "And what," he murmured down at her, "could possibly scare them about you?"

She snuggled into him as easily as if she were meant to be there. He tightened his hold on her. Damn, but this felt good. "Because I'm so clumsy," she admitted. "Because I hurt people."

"They're idiots," said Jon.

In his arms Grace shivered. He turned so that his back was to the open window, thinking he should probably close it, but not wanting to let go of her to do so.

"Are you all right?" he asked.

She nodded vehemently, only hitting his chin with her head once before she tipped her pretty face back up toward his. Her blue eyes glittered with tears, but she was smiling. "I wish you weren't going," she said. "I don't feel so clumsy around you."

Damn. He winced, hating to hurt either of them further.

Then Grace said, "But I understand if you want to go be with the other squirrels."

Jon felt a slow smile stretch his mouth. Sure, he'd rather she compared him to a manlier wild animal than a squirrel. A bear, maybe. A cougar.

But the fact was, she was letting him go freely.

"You are some kind of treasure, Grace Sullivan," he murmured, ducking his head closer to hers. "Someone's going to see your true color and appreciate you the way you deserve to be appreciated."

"How's that?" she whispered.

So he kissed her again.

Maybe he shouldn't. The rules of society surely forbade it, but he didn't give a wooden nickel for the rules of society. His gratitude to Patrick Sullivan forbade it . . . but he'd fought taking anything from Sullivan from the beginning. And as for Grace—

She returned his kiss with an enthusiasm that made it completely acceptable. One kiss become two, became three, sweet and free and all but humming with happiness. She wrapped her arms tighter around his waist, her fingers clutching at his shirt, and pressed herself to him with undisguised enthusiasm.

This was what kissing had been invented for: tasting her, breathing her, feeling her through his whole body. But Jon's own enthusiasm was going to be increasingly difficult to disguise if they weren't careful. So he continued kissing her, but eased just one hobbled step back so that her warm curves weren't nestled quite so intimately against the front of him.

Grace pressed forward, her bodice a forbidden pillow against his ribs, her skirts brushing tantalizingly against the increasingly wonderful, embarrassing tension beneath Jon's belt. Then she was pressing against him with even more than skirts; he could feel the warm pressure of her belly . . .

His body responded with enthusiasm, as if there would be anything more between them, so to speak, than these last delicious kisses. There would not, Jon sternly told his body. This was good-bye. Grace Sullivan was a good girl, kisses aside, not some floozy in a farmer's-daughter story.

With almost superhuman strength, Jon stumbled back just a little bit, away from the delicious press of her body.

The back of his thighs hit the windowjamb.

Grace surged forward, into his arms yet again, and Jon lost his balance. *Uff do.*

At least he managed to let go of Grace as he tumbled out the window. Somehow, he managed to turn to try to catch himself, to try to protect his injured leg . . .

He felt as much as heard the wrench when his hand hit the edge of the porch as he bounced off it, into a five-foot snowdrift. *This is going to hurt,* he thought, lying facedown in the snow. He was sorry to hear Grace's cry of dismay above him, sorry to have scared her again.

But at least the snow took care of that wonderful, embarrassing tension he'd been so worried about Grace noticing.

She'd done it again.

Grace waited miserably in the family room, with Mama and Comtesse Arabella, while Da and the doctor saw to Jon's hurt wrist in the parlor. She found little consolation in the fact that Belle and Charisma had gone out with their fiancés before this latest disaster. They would find out soon enough.

Rather, they would hear the lie Jon had told as Da helped him back inside, that he'd spun and lost his balance when he heard Grace drop her tray outside his room. She'd wanted to cry when she heard that, heard him lie to protect her, except that she was already too near tears from the reality that she'd done it again.

She'd broken him. One minute they'd been kissing, and she'd been miserable that he was leaving but so very, very happy with his kisses. The next minute she'd pushed him out a third-story window.

If the snowdrifts hadn't been so high, he might not have survived!

"It's all right, pet," said Mama, taking Grace's hand in hers. "The man ought not to have been so jumpy that a simple spill of crockery would send him out the window. He ought not have had the window open in the first place! This is not your fault."

But it was. And if Grace told her mother how very much it was, then Da would send Jon away despite this latest injury! So she stayed silent and miserable.

Especially when Jon cried out in the other room.

A glimpse of movement from the edge of her vision drew Grace's attention to a curly black head peeking past the corner of the family room archway. Wide, concerned black eyes met hers.

She widened her eyes back at little Gio. *It's all right,* she mouthed—the same words her mother had used. Then, because the little boy shouldn't be alone, she added a silent *Go see Cook.*

At least, she'd thought she was being silent. Her mother said, "What's that, Grace?"

Grace jumped, startled. "I should go see Phronsy. Tell her I broke the coffee urn."

"This is ridiculous," exclaimed Comtesse Arabella. "Whatever were you doing, behaving like some kind of servant for zat man in ze first place?"

"Arabella," protested Mama.

"No, Marie, I'll not keep silent. You brought me here to attempt—to *struggle*—to turn zis girl into a young lady of breeding and comportment. Bad enough that she has yet to master anything so simple as dancing, or ze finer arts, without leaving chaos in her wake. But when she zen uses her spare time delivering coffee to a lowly miner—as a favor to ze cook yet—"

"He's not a lowly miner!" The words escaped Grace before she knew they would, but facing her beautifully dressed mentor, she felt good to have said them. Even if her mother *was* staring at her. "I mean, yes, of course Mr. Erikson is a miner. But so was Da, not that awfully long ago, and look where that got us."

The *comtesse* said, "It's nothing to be proud of, Miss Sullivan."

"Well, it's nothing to be embarrassed about, either!" Grace looked at her mother as she said that.

Mama looked thoughtful but said, "You'll be respecting your elders better than that, Grace Sullivan."

And of course, she had a point. As quickly as Grace's moment of rebellion came upon her, it drained away. *Honor thy mother and father.* It was in the Bible and everything. "Yes, ma'am."

"The *comtesse* is quite right that you've better things to do with your time than behave like a common waitress."

As opposed to a domestic, like Bridey had been? But Grace wasn't sure she could have dared ask that, even if the moment of rebellion had stayed. "Yes, ma'am."

"You'll not be keeping company with that young man," insisted Mama, which is when Grace realized just how close her dismay had come to giving her away. Giving Jon away. Causing more trouble than broken dishes or spilled food. "He is your father's guest, not ours."

Grace thought about how Jon had held her, had kissed her. She thought about how he'd lied to protect her, never letting on that she'd been in his room, that she'd managed to push him out the window because they'd been kissing so . . . enthusiastically.

She thought about how he'd winced with pain as Da helped him limp in the back door, and how Da had packed his wrist with ice while sending for the doctor.

She thought of how difficult a time he would have with the crutches, now that he'd hurt his wrist. He'd need to stay awhile longer, whether he wanted to run off to the mountains or not. She didn't want to be happy for that, but she was. So at least she could do something for him in return.

She looked her mother in the eye and said, "Yes, ma'am. I have to prepare for the Founder's Day ball, anyway."

Jon Erikson wasn't the only person who could lie.

Chapter Eleven

"There," said Euphrosyne, brushing her hands off amid the shimmering mists of the alternate dimension of Mount Olympus. "I believe there can be no question that my charges have strong feelings for each other."

"Feelings?" Thalia, archetype of charm, pursed her lips slightly. "I do hate to disagree, sister, but the kind of feelings young Erikson has for Grace Sullivan may have more to do with her willingness to kiss him than with any sense of true and permanent love."

"There is nothing wrong with those feelings as well," admitted Euphrosyne. "Although compared to your charges, and to Aglaia's, I believe Jon and Grace to be the soul of decorum."

"They would make a handsome couple," admitted Aglaia, archetype of beauty, as she lounged back on a cloud. "But all our matches have managed that. It is true, dear, that Grace seems somewhat more willing to disobey her mother for this man. But Jon seems as anxious to leave in pursuit of adventure as he ever has."

"Yet he's staying," said Euphrosyne.

Aglaia shook her head. "Only because he has little choice, dear. Neither I nor Thalia had to resort to actually injuring our charges."

Thalia was quick to soften her sister's bluntness. "Euphrosyne is not the one hurting poor Mr. Erikson. That would be Grace."

"Do you think so?" Euphrosyne reached behind a soaring Doric column and picked just a little ambrosia—just enough to add something extra nice to Grace's next cooking project. She would tell the girl it was nutmeg. "Perhaps you should pay closer attention, dears. . . ."

"Did she do it on purpose?" asked Gio from the foot of the bed, eyes wide at the importance of Jon's new injury. "To keep you here?"

"Of course she didn't do it on purpose!" Jon scowled at how that came out. Whiskey might help muffle some of the pain throbbing up his arm, but it didn't do a lot for his speaking abilities. "She didn't do it at all. I'm the one who fell out the window."

"Does it hurt?" The kid came around the bed and leaned forward to poke a skinny finger toward Jon's bandaged hand.

Jon swung his injured paw away from the kid, not bothering to give him the tough-man "what, this?" treatment. "Of course it hurts. Sprains *hurt.*"

"But it is not broken?"

"No. Give me another week, two at the most, and I'm still leaving. Get used to it."

"You are grumpy," decided Gio.

"I was this close to getting out." Jon used his uninjured hand to make a pinching gesture, to illustrate just how close he'd been. "*This close.* And now . . ."

Gio scowled, lower lip protruding.

"Hey." Jon sat up, leaned precariously forward, and flicked a finger lightly across the kid's button nose. "You are one of the two reasons I'm glad to be here another week."

Gio's lashes lifted to meet his gaze, to test the truth of his words. Jon guessed the truth must be there, even through the haze of Patrick Sullivan's good whiskey, because the kid grinned broadly. "I bet I know what the other reason is, yes?"

It was a bet Jon wouldn't take. "You probably do. Yes."

"She smells good," said Gio.

Jon leaned back in the pillows, remembering. Grace had smelled of fresh coffee and warm cinnamon and soap, and of the fresh mountain air that had wafted around them through that treacherous open window. Heaven. "Yeah. She does."

"And she's soft."

"Yeah. She is." All over, but especially where women *should* be round and soft. Her lips had felt as soft as buttermilk against his. And her hips pressing against his . . .

Jon noticed Gio looking intrigued, and frowned at him. "And you shouldn't be talking about how soft a lady is."

Gio shrugged. "I just mean, I understand why you like her."

You couldn't comprehend the half of it, thought Jon, worried.

He'd never fallen so hard for a woman in his life.

And that wasn't counting the three stories.

* * *

"May I sit beside you for the lecture, Miss Grace?"

It was Robert James, of the Denver Jameses. Grace had been standing very still in the lyceum hall, trying not to touch or hurt anything. For a moment she almost forgot that she could move, even to answer the gentleman's request.

But Charisma nudged her as a reminder.

"Thank you," Grace said. "That's very kind of you."

She noticed Charisma and Belle exchanging excited glances, both with each other and with their fiancés. She tried to feel excited herself. Robert James was exactly the kind of man Mama wanted Grace to marry. He was wealthy, sophisticated, and an established member of society. As she accepted the arm he offered—not even punching him accidentally in the ribs or getting her hand caught in his frock coat—Grace noticed that Mr. James had a kind face and was even rather handsome.

For a man with brown hair.

His arm felt solid beneath her hand, and she did not care. He did not have honey gold hair. He did not have summertime blue eyes. His smile, while pleasant, did not light feelings in her chest like a match to kindling wood.

Not the way Jon's did.

"You should care," she whispered to herself. Even if Jon Erikson *were* a proper beau for her, which he was not. Even if he *had* kissed her in a way that, even now, made her want to squirm on the lyceum hall's wooden bench—which he ought not to have done.

She had knocked him out a third-floor window. She doubted he would be wanting to kiss her again anytime soon.

"I am anxious for spring to arrive," said Mr. James, to make polite conversation. "Don't you agree?"

But when spring arrived, Jon would be gone.

So she said, "Oh, the lecture's about to start."

The speaker was a representative of the New York City Society for the Prevention of Cruelty to Children. He spoke of how a founding member had come across a child, beaten terribly. He had found no fitting laws by which to protect her except statutes against animal cruelty. Thus, he began his crusade to awaken interest in the abuses to which many children were exposed "by the intemperance, cruelty, or cupidity of parents and guardians."

Grace, imagining little Gio from Jon's room, sat up with growing interest. She wished she'd learned more of the child's story before, well . . . before kissing Jon, then pushing him out the window.

Mr. James leaned nearer her and whispered, "I hope you don't find me too forward, Miss Grace. . . ."

She glanced at him, then quickly back at the speaker, who'd just said something about immigrant children. Gio had an accent like an immigrant child. "What was that?"

"Too forward," Mr. James repeated.

Grace said, "I'd really like to listen to this, Mr. James."

The gentleman beside her sat back, and she was able to hear more about the plight of abused children . . . and to feel increasingly impatient to get back to the house and make sure Gio was all right.

She did not notice Belle's stiff posture, on her other side, until the carriage ride home.

"He was going to ask you to the Founder's Day ball," Belle said.

For a moment, Grace did not know who she meant. The speaker? Gio?

Jon?

Then she understood. "Mr. James?"

"Of course Mr. James."

To the Founder's Day ball? "You can't know that."

Belle said, "Yes, I can, because he talked to Kit and Will about it. They said you would be receptive, but now you've made them liars. Mr. James was going to ask you to the ball, and you *told him to be quiet*. I would have expected as much from Charisma—"

"Hey!" protested Charisma.

"At one time," qualified Belle. "But not from you, Grace."

Oh. Grace knew she should feel bad for having missed that opportunity. And she did feel, well, guilty. Everyone wanted it for her, after all.

But she did not feel bad at all. Despite the guilt, she felt vaguely relieved. "No," she said slowly. "You would have expected me to step on his foot, or fall onto him, or trip him. But I didn't do any of that, did I?"

Both her sisters stared at this unexpected announcement.

"Actually," said Charisma as the carriage stopped in front of their tall house, "you didn't."

Belle's bright smile made up for her earlier scolding. "You didn't do any of that, Grace. Comtesse Arabella's lessons are working!"

That had to be it, of course. Especially if the *comtesse* really was Grace's fairy godmother . . . or whoever it was that the Three Graces monument was sending to help the Sullivan girls. Grace's guilt intensified. Having Comtesse Arabella here should be the best thing in her life, and instead she'd been resenting the woman's instruction and crediting her brief moments of poise to, well . . . to Jon.

To Jon, and the fact that she'd made round pancakes in his presence.

"The lessons are working," she echoed, trying to muster the enthusiasm her sisters so clearly felt.

"By the Founder's Day ball, I wouldn't be surprised if you are as well matched as Charisma and I." When the carriage door was opened by the groom, Belle let the man help her out. She was the oldest, after all. Charisma went next.

"By the Founder's Day ball," said Grace, imagining herself on the arm of Mr. Robert James. Her mother would be vindicated. Her father would forgive her mother for interfering. Everyone would be happy, even her.

Wouldn't she?

When the groom took her hand to help her out of the carriage, Grace absently took it, leaned out the door . . .

And fell on him.

"No, you did not knock me out the window," repeated Jon. He'd lost count of how often he'd had to tell Grace that over the past week, how often she'd apologized. She seemed determined to take blame for his clumsiness. "I sort of . . . well . . . backed out of it."

"Because of me." She stood just inside the doorway, her arms wrapped around herself. Part of it was because she was a good girl and knew she should not be in his room, so she was compromising by being *barely* in his room. Part of it was, he suspected, because he stood by the slightly open window. "Just like poor Sam."

Sam was apparently the man in charge of the Sullivans' stables. From what Jon had heard of the story—partly from Grace and mostly from Gio— the man had botched helping Grace from the carriage after her lyceum the other night, and ended up with a broken nose.

"That's it," Jon decided, pushing away from the wall. "Come here and get on the bed."

Grace's eyes widened adorably. "Excuse me?"

He hobbled closer to her, with the help of the bedpost, then held out his good hand. "I'm going to prove something to you. Stand on the bed."

"Mr. Erikson, I cannot be caught on your bed!"

"That, Miss Sullivan," he said, reaching past her, "is why we're closing the door. It's not as if we don't have a chaperon."

Little Gio sat at the head of the bed, eating one of the pastries Grace had brought from the kitchen, watching the two adults with clear interest. Even so, Grace jumped when the door clicked shut behind her.

And, true, Jon stood right beside her. In fact, with his arm behind her on the door, he was one quick movement from drawing it around her and pulling her to him.

Remembering the last time he'd done that, he ached to pull her to him again.

Remembering the three-story fall into the snow, and the different kind of ache in his wrist, he reined in that ungentlemanly reaction. Despite how close they now stood. Despite how her lips parted in something close to awe as she looked up at him.

She swallowed hard and said, "I don't think little boys make proper guardians."

"I don't know about you," teased Jon, "but I'm less likely to misbehave with the kid looking on."

As he'd hoped, that got her Irish up. "I am no more likely to misbehave than you are!"

"Then why worry that the door's closed?"

"Because of how it looks!"

Damn, but society rules could be wearying.

"What's more important?" challenged Jon. "How something looks, or how it is?"

Gio, from the bed, said, "Why does it matter?" His words sounded muffled.

Without even looking at him, Jon said, "Don't talk with your mouth full."

Amusingly, Grace said the same thing. They shared a quick smile, and she ducked her head. "And the answer, Gio, is how something is. That's got to be more important. But it doesn't mean how something looks doesn't also signify."

"This is just to make a point," Jon said. "Fine, if you won't get on the bed, try this. Try pushing me."

She blinked up at him. "What?"

"I'm going to stand here, and you try to push me

over. If you can, I'll admit that you're the terror you like to think you are. But if you can't, you're going to stand on that bed and let me demonstrate that Sam's just a lousy groom."

"But—Jon, you're hurt! You've got a broken leg and a sprained wrist. . . ." He could tell by the way her gaze clouded as she cataloged his injuries that she was starting to assume blame again.

So he pushed her. Just barely. On the shoulder. "Dare you."

Her eyes and mouth widened.

Gio, behind him, laughed.

"Come on," said Jon, nudging her again. Just a little. Just enough to make her take a step backward. "Push me back."

Just as he'd hoped, she planted a hand against his chest and . . .

Well, she planted a hand against his chest, anyway. Then she pulled it back. "I don't want to hurt you."

"You won't." He turned and hobbled back a step or two. "Here, I'll stand against the bed. That way, if you do push me over, I'll land on a feather mattress. All right?"

She bit her lower lip, clearly torn. She glanced worriedly at the closed door to the hallway behind her.

"Chicken," said Jon.

Grace's eyes widened as she looked back. "I am not!"

"Yes, you are. You besmirch my manliness; then you won't even let me prove myself. All I'm asking is that you try to push me over. It can't be that hard, can it? You've been terrorizing everyone else for years by accident, haven't you? So just for once, on purpose, why don't you—"

She rushed him.

He braced his one good leg.

She ran into him. Hard. Hard enough to force a soft "Oof!" out of him.

But he didn't fall. "See?"

Grace planted both hands against his chest and pushed.

Jon liked feeling her spread hands through his chambray shirt. He'd like it even more without the shirt, but of course, that was out of the question. Even if the kid weren't here. "Is that all you've got?"

She tried using her shoulder to knock him over. But Grace was a small woman. He was a big guy. And he'd had several weeks to get used to compensating for his bum leg.

"Can't do it, can you?"

She looked up, her frustration slowly melting to . . . what? Relief? Joy? "No," she said. "I can't."

Gio said, "Now you must get onto the bed. That was the bargain."

The kid was easily entertained.

Grace blushed, but Jon didn't give her a chance to think this out too long. "*Stand* on the bed," he clarified, offering her a hand up. "Just long enough for me to demonstrate something about Sam."

To his delight, she put her hand in his, gathered her skirts with her free hand, and leaped like a mountain goat onto his bed. Her feet sank into the feather mattress that held him each night, up to the tops of her high-top leather shoes, and her stockings today were blue.

Jon had to close his eyes for a moment in order

to break the spell of those shapely calves and make himself look away. "Uh, okay," he said, clearing his throat. "Let's pretend that you're home from your lyceum. So . . ." He slanted his gaze back to her, playful. "What are you wearing?"

She looked down at herself and her nicely tailored green dress and blue pinafore, confused.

Gio, a little sharper at the moment, said, "She is wearing a dress of crispy gold material that rustles when she walks, like this. *Shhh. Shhh.* The material inside her cape matches it. It looks very nice on her."

Both Jon and Grace slowly turned to look at the boy.

Jon asked, "Where, exactly, were you hiding when you saw this?"

"The third-floor landing." Gio took another bite of pastry. "Why?"

Thank goodness the boy hadn't taken to invading the Sullivan girls' bedrooms! Jon saw a similar relief in Grace's expression when she looked back at him.

"That is what I wore to the lyceum," she admitted. "There were shiny buttons on the shoulders. Comtesse Arabella wanted me to wear my mother's pearls, but we just couldn't risk it."

"Couldn't risk you losing them?"

"Breaking them." She bit her lip again momentarily. "You would be surprised how many people can fall down if you scatter a whole necklace full of pearls across the floor, all at once. I know."

Gio laughed.

Jon scowled at him, then looked back to Grace. "Okay, so you're wearing this gold-colored gown and your cape, right? And gloves and a hat and all that. I bet you looked wonderful."

And he did. He wished he could have seen her. He wondered how low-cut the gown had been.

When she smiled at the compliment, he guessed she couldn't have looked any prettier than she did right now.

"I'm going to be Sam," he said now, pretending to open the imaginary carriage door. "Why, welcome home, Miss Grace. Watch your step. Now, fall on me."

Grace blinked down at him. "He didn't say that."

Jon rolled his eyes. "That wasn't Sam; that was me. I want you to pretend you're getting out of the carriage and fall on me like you did Sam."

"But . . . I *like* your nose."

He grinned at the wistful note in her voice. "I'm glad to hear that, Grace. I like yours, too. But both our noses are safe, promise."

She hesitated.

"We had a deal," he warned, and again offered his good hand. "Welcome home, Miss Grace. Watch your step."

She took a deep breath, stepped toward him, then plunged.

Jon caught her around the waist with his arm, held her against him, and eased her to the floor. "There."

She stared up at him, eyes wide and bright, as if he were strong and wonderful and . . . and important.

Worse, he wanted to be important.

"There," he repeated, still holding her somewhat

tightly against his side. "That's what he should have done."

"But . . . maybe he's not as strong as you."

"He didn't have a broken leg and a sprained wrist, either."

Grace narrowed her eyes, then declared, "Let's do it again. Just to be sure."

But when Jon helped her hop onto the bed again and she flopped off it at him, the result was the same. Oh, he didn't catch her with a lot of finesse. She shifted on his hip some, and her petticoats bunched as she slid gently to the floor. But nobody got hurt.

Unless you counted the increased chances that one or both of them could be badly hurt if they didn't stop staring at each other like this. If they acted on the attraction roiling between them. If he still left, without her . . . or worse, if he had to stay.

"Now me!" demanded Gio, like a good chaperon. "Do me!"

Jon grinned apologetically down at Grace.

She smiled adoringly back up at him.

Worse, he liked it.

Gio jumped up and down on the bed, catching their attention, so Jon turned to him and said, "Welcome home, Mr. Gio. Watch your step."

The kid launched himself off the bed, and Jon scooped him one-handed onto his shoulder before tossing him back onto the bed.

Gio squealed with laughter.

Grace's and Jon's hands collided as they covered the boy's mouth. "Shhh!"

Then Gio, in retaliation, tickled them. Jon jumped, and *Grace* squealed with laughter.

Jon's one good hand was busy with Gio.

So instead of covering her mouth, he kissed her. So much for chaperons. Gio stopped laughing, which freed Jon's good hand to cup Grace's cheek as he deepened the kiss. Grace definitely stopped laughing. By the way she surged up into the kiss, though, she wasn't dissatisfied.

A sudden pounding on the door startled them apart. Grace's elbow somehow jabbed sharply into Jon's wrapped wrist as they spun away from each other, and he bit back a groan at the shock of pain rather than let her hear it. Her, or anyone else.

"Erikson! Are you sleeping?"

Her father!

Chapter Twelve

Despite the many slips and missteps that stained her life, Grace had never realized just how quickly one could plunge from sheer joy to complete horror.

Da!

He would catch her alone in Jon's room and send Jon away. Or else he'd catch her with Gio, and both send Jon away and send Gio to an orphanage. Either way, her father would be horrified by her behavior. Comtesse Arabella would likely refuse to help such a hoyden. Belle and Charisma would be embarrassed. Mama would blame Da for bringing Jon into their home.

Either way, Jon would be turned out. Forever. And she might never feel as happy as she had when he kissed her.

The awfulness of those possibilities stunned her so thoroughly that, when a small hand tugged her backward, Grace followed without question. Only when she realized what little Gio was doing—tugging her into the empty wardrobe—did her brain start to work again.

This was wrong. She couldn't possibly spy on her father! And yet . . .

And yet she scrambled quickly up onto a stack of drawers, pulling her feet up after her. She supposed kissing and lying weren't the only sins she would commit for the sake of Jon Erikson—not because he asked her to, but because she wanted to. She scooped an armful of her skirt into the armoire while Gio landed in her lap and pulled the door shut, giving her one last glimpse of the bedroom door starting to open. . . .

And of Jon watching both of them with wide eyes, even less comfortable with secrecy than Grace.

For the first time, Grace felt glad Jon kept his duffel bag out in the room, always ready to go.

"Erikson," said her father's familiar voice, thick with his Irish brogue. "Did you not hear me, boy?"

"Uh . . ."

Gio's soft face pressed close to Grace's cheek, and the boy whispered, "He is not very good at this, yes?"

Yet one more reason she liked Jon so much.

Jon said, "That noise you may have heard . . ."

Da said, "Noise?"

Now that Grace thought about it, Da's hearing wasn't the best in the household. Charisma once said it was because he'd worked so much with explosives in his youth—and that employers demanding such dangerous work should take extra precautions to protect their workers' ears. Charisma was full of radical, wonderful ideas like that.

Jon quickly said, "Never mind."

"I reckoned you might be getting a touch of cabin fever since your latest fall," said Da. "I know I do, of late, and 'tis me own house. Or so says the deed."

"It, uh, hasn't been that bad."

Grace smiled when Jon said that. Her lips still tingled from his kiss, after all. His being here hadn't been bad at all; it had been wonderful!

Well . . . except that she was not progressing with her lady lessons as she should. And, yes, she was currently hiding in an armoire with a small orphan boy. She supposed that didn't count as *good*.

Perhaps her father felt equally relieved. "Might you consider staying in Colorado Springs, then?" he asked. "I could always use a good foreman in my mines, and I'm not ashamed to tell you, I've enjoyed your company. Of late, the only folks Bridey wants to keep around us are either servants or snobs."

Oh, dear. Grace's stomach clenched at the familiar refrain.

Jon said, "Stanton and Barclay seem like good men."

"True enough," agreed Da, and Grace let out a breath she'd been holding.

Shifting her weight more comfortably, she whispered to Gio, "He's wonderful."

Gio whispered, "Your papa?"

"It seems Belle and Charisma found good enough fellows," continued her father, "though I can't wholly approve of how their matches got made."

Grace thought, *What?*

Jon said, "Excuse me?"

Da said, "No, 'tis not for any but family ears, that tale. But I do fear for my Gracie."

"Uh . . . Grace?" repeated Jon. "That would, uh, be your youngest, right?"

Gio giggled softly. He smelled a lot like Jon did—like the same soap, Grace realized—but less solid. More cuddly.

She hugged him.

"That gussied-up prig Bridey brought in to citify Gracie is an embarrassment! But the woman won't hear reason. She's set herself on having society sons-in-law, no matter if she has to sacrifice her own children to do it. Damn, but there's times I wish the Grace of God hadn't ever showed color, and we could've lived and died poor and happy."

Grace's mouth fell open in the darkness, and she leaned closer to the door to hear better. Her Da wished he hadn't struck it rich?

Jon said, "Uhm . . . God moves in mysterious ways?"

"Eh?" Then, apparently, Da understood. "'Tis the name of me first claim, boy, up the mountain from here. I called the mine the Grace of God because . . . well, 'twas a fondness, of sorts, that name. I proposed to my Bridey in the Garden of the Gods, near the rock spires folks call the Three Graces. That's why we named the girls as we did, and why we called my mine the Grace of God."

"He still loves her," whispered Grace, mainly to herself, in the wardrobe.

Da said, "Damn, but she gave it up prettily, she did."

Grace's face burned. He couldn't mean . . . !

Maybe Jon feared the same thing, because he didn't say a word. Then, to her deep relief, Da continued, "That claim all but handed me my first real silver; then she just kept giving more. By the time she dried up on me, I'd already invested in more mines and became the so-called silver king you see today. For all the good it does me."

Jon said, "It can't be that bad . . . can it?"

"Aye, boy, it can. The wife takes trips to Europe and invites over guests I can't stand the sight of, all in the name of almighty culture. The girls get shelved away into different rooms of their own, if you can imagine it, in a house so large I hardly know where they are, even when the whole lot of us are home. It leads to trouble, especially with Bridey all but throwing the girls at her society men."

Grace, wondering what kind of trouble, pressed her ear closer to the door—and heard an ominous click. A thin line of light appeared before her, running across her and Gio. *The latch was giving way!*

Worse, she was starting to lose her balance.

She spread her hands against the wardrobe wall, trying to hold herself, and Gio, up. Gio caught at the inside of the door, but even his little fingers were too large to get a good hold on its edge without opening it farther.

"*Uff da,*" he whispered, sounding like Jon but with an Italian accent.

Grace's father said, "I've told nobody this, Erikson, but last summer I was angry enough with my wife to consider moving out. She'd paid men— *paid them*—to escort our daughters . . . Ah, never mind the reason. Just know that, as I was pondering my choices, I rode up to the Grace of God. I'd boarded her up, back when Bridey talked me into giving up the dirt mining to wear a suit and oversee matters instead; I'd rather let the mine guard her secrets than hire someone else to violate the old girl."

Gio caught his breath—and with a slight squeak, the wardrobe door slid open another half inch. Despite struggling to keep her tipping balance, Grace could now see her father's back, wearing shirtsleeves and a vest. Her mother would be angry that he didn't have on his frock coat, but not as angry as she'd be at Grace's falling out of Jon Erikson's wardrobe!

She could also see Jon's summertime blue eyes widen when he saw what was happening.

"I went into that mine, boy, and I missed it, like I would once have thought I would miss my wife. The deep-earth coolness. The scent. And I felt the stone, and I thought, *There's more down here.* Surely you know that feeling, that certainty that the color's calling to you."

"Uh, yes, sir." Jon began to edge toward the wardrobe, but Da turned with him, so Jon quickly stopped. "I mean, I haven't been all that certain about any mine, or I would have stayed. But I hope to feel that, someday. Once I move on."

Grace felt her fingers start to squeak across the wall of the wardrobe, beginning to lose their battle with gravity. The door slid open another half inch.

"'Tis the difference between us, boy," sighed Da, shaking his head. "The joys of your life are ahead of you, and the joys of mine . . ."

He couldn't mean it, could he? Grace tried to dig her fingernails into the wood, as much to hear what else her father meant to say as to keep from being discovered. Gio's weight in her lap pulled her inexorably downward.

Jon said, "You can't mean that, Mr. Sullivan." But he sounded distracted.

"I do, boy. You still dream of finding the claim that will yield unimaginable riches. I've found her and have disliked it so much that, sure though I am the Grace of God has more to give, I'd slit my wrists before I'd mine her."

Grace was so horrified, her grip on the wardrobe wall slipped. The door, and she, and Gio all began to lean out into the room . . .

And Jon, in one big bound, jumped closer to them and slammed it shut with his shoulder. The latch snicked securely shut. On the other side of the door, Grace heard him chuckle unconvincingly. "Lost my balance," he said.

"At least you've good reason for it," said Da. "At least your leg will heal. I lost my balance so slowly, so quietly, that I don't know if I'll e'er find it again. All I know for certain is, I've got to do what's best for the girls. No matter what their mother says."

Gio whispered, "I do not understand. He does not want the silver in his mine?"

Grace didn't know how to explain it to him. She wasn't sure she could explain it to herself. She felt too sick to try.

"Well," Jon's voice said cheerfully, "Miss Belle and Miss Charisma seem pretty well matched. That's got to relieve you. Some."

"You've never had children." Da didn't make it sound like a happy thing. "You cannot understand. As long as I've fear for my Gracie's happiness, matters cannot rest. And if that woman leads her into misery . . ."

"You mean the *comtesse?*" asked Jon.

"I mean," said Da, "me wife."

Jon had never seen a man so low, and he had no idea what to say. All he knew was that he had to keep holding this wardrobe door shut and trying to look innocent.

He didn't feel innocent, not with the man's youngest daughter pressed up against the other side of the door he leaned upon. Not having already taken liberties with her that should at the very least get him tossed from the man's house, and possibly beaten on the way out.

"Sir," he said, "I'm really not sure you should be telling any of this to me." Or to Grace. Or to Gio, for that matter.

If the man weren't so distracted, surely he'd have noticed something amiss.

Sullivan sighed. "You're right, of course. I'm an old fool to bring my troubles to you, and you already sufferin' from enough of your own. Forgive me."

Now Jon felt even worse. Forgive *him?* "I didn't mean . . . that is . . ."

"Nay, I'll let you get back to your rest," insisted Paddy Sullivan; then he paused. "How do you keep yourself from going mad up here?"

By playing with a child you don't know about, and kissing your youngest daughter.

Jon smiled weakly. "I read?"

"Never was much of a reader myself," admitted

Sullivan, shaking his head as he walked toward the door. "Yet somethin' else that mortifies my wife, though she hardly seemed to mind it when first we met."

If the man told him anything more about his personal life, Jon thought he might throw himself out the window again.

After making sure the wardrobe latch held.

"Well, if there be any books you're wantin' and cannot get from Bridey's fancy-schmancy library, let me know." To Jon's relief, Patrick reached the doorway. "I'd like my money to be used for causes that make sense now and then, as well as the foolish ones."

"I'll be sure to do that, sir."

"And as soon as you're able to handle those crutches again, join the family for dinner. There'll be no further accusations like before." He meant the stolen silver.

"Thank you, sir," said Jon. "I'll do that. Once my wrist is strong enough for the crutches."

And finally, with a nod, Grace's father left. He didn't close the door behind him, so Jon had to hobble quietly to the doorway and look out, to make sure the man had gone down the stairs, before closing the door himself. He hobbled back to open the armoire.

Gio and Grace fell out in a heap, on top of him.

He caught Grace. Gio, like most little boys, bounced.

"Are you all right?" Jon asked Grace, setting her onto her feet.

"That was awful," she said, and her wide eyes emphasized the sentiment. "He sounded so unhappy."

"Yeah." Jon glanced toward the door through which Mr. Sullivan had left. "He did."

Gio, hopping onto the bed, asked, "How could he be unhappy? He is rich."

"Money isn't everything," said Jon. Then he thought, *Unless you're Mrs. Sullivan.*

But he didn't dare say that in front of Grace.

"But it helps," said Gio. "It pays the doctor."

Grace smoothed her skirts with shaking hands, glancing toward the armoire that had hidden her. "I have to go. I shouldn't have heard any of that."

Jon said, "You wanted to leave the door to the hall open. I'm the one who made you come farther in."

He was also the one who'd kissed her. Again. But he felt funny mentioning that, if she wasn't going to.

She backed away from him and Gio both. "I have to go. I have to learn how to be a lady, so that my da can see I'm happy despite Mama's . . . I mean, that Mama's helped make me happy."

Jon stared. "By learning how to be a lady?"

It wouldn't be his first choice of how to make either her or her father happy. But Grace nodded vehemently. "Last summer, when Mama paid those men to escort Belle, Charisma, and me to the Garden of the Gods like Da said, something happened. Something . . . unusual. We made wishes, and they already came true for my sisters. It's as if it's . . . as if it's a bargain I have to keep. If I only trust in it, everything just has to work out. I'm sorry if I can't spend as much time with you."

She'd reached the door, and Jon wished he knew what to say to stop her. He also knew he had no right to involve himself in her life, not any more than he already had.

She looked at Gio, clearly miserable. "I'm sorry."

The little boy glanced from her to Jon, and—when Jon said nothing—he glanced back. "But . . . but your papa said he would bring books. If Jon asks, he can bring books about mining, yes?"

"Well . . ." She hesitated. "Yes. I suppose he can get books on mining."

"We both want to learn about mining," declared Gio.

Jon had a bad feeling about this. "You don't need to know anything about mining."

"I do! Even if you don't take me with you, I will someday be a miner, too, and I need to know!" Gio's usually bright, dark eyes took on a slow thoughtfulness that made Jon even more nervous than his rebellion. "And I need Miss Grace to read them to me."

Grace opened her mouth to protest but couldn't seem to find the voice.

"Please?" wheedled Gio. "Just a little. You are educated, yes? You can read."

Jon said, "She's not the only one."

Gio said, "But you do the big words wrong. And you cannot turn the pages."

What a little stinker! Except . . . almost too late, Jon noticed that the little boy seemed to be silently trying to tell him something. Something like *Be quiet, you big Norwegian.* Something like *You want her to come back, too.*

And he did want her to come back. So he said, "In a few days, I'm sure my wrist will be fine for page-turning."

Gio turned his dark gaze of need back to poor Grace, and she didn't stand a chance.

"Fine," she said. "I'll check our library, and if I can't find any books on mining, Jon can ask Da to get some. Then I'll come read to you. When I'm not practicing my feminine comportment, I mean. Now, I really must—"

But she *oof*ed to a stop when Gio flung his arms around her waist and hugged her. Then she hugged him back.

Jon looked at them together and felt something warm and satisfied . . . and wholly inappropriate. He was leaving. Soon. Leaving the woman. Leaving the kid.

But the idea felt far less like a promise than a warning to himself.

A warning that might be coming way too late.

Chapter Thirteen

"This," said Belle, with Kit Stanhope beside her, "is bound to help, Grace. We should have taught it to you months ago."

Grace looked at the selection of fans spread across the parlor table. Belle had collected so many since Kit had begun courting her the previous year. Some were painted paper or wood, and some were cloth—silk, and velvet, and brocade. Some had lace, and some had feathers. All of them looked beautiful . . . and delicate. "I thought you were afraid I'd break them."

Belle hesitated.

Kit Stanhope smoothly said, "They're mere fans, even if you should. But let's not think the worst, shall we?"

Grace nodded, determined at least to try. Jon didn't believe her to be inordinately clumsy, did he? And she very much trusted Jon.

In fact, she wished she were upstairs in his room right now. Normally, she spent mornings with him, since Comtesse Arabella slept so very late. But this morning, Belle and Kit had made a special effort to teach her the perfect method by which to win Robert James's attentions.

Reminding herself that she *wanted* Robert James's attentions, if only to avert disaster between her parents, Grace dutifully turned her attention back to the lesson.

Belle said, "The best way to use a fan is as an extension of your hand. It can help communicate your emotions." To illustrate, she showed Grace several expressions, all of them complemented by the fan. She snapped it angrily, fingered it with intrigue, even let it fall carelessly off her fingertips to show how very bored she was pretending to be. Kit and Grace both watched in fascination until Belle extended a silk-and-ivory fan toward her fiancé and drew it lightly down his angled cheek.

His smile spread as she did. "Now, now, darling. Be good."

"Then you explain," teased Belle.

So Kit did. "I learned the language of the fan in Paris, just last year. There are perhaps thirty different signals one can send without saying a word. Since Belle taught it to Colorado Springs society, it is highly likely that Robert James will understand several of the more obvious movements, such as . . . a confirmation of friendship."

Belle dropped her fan and looked mildly dismayed. Grace was unsure if that was part of the lesson, until Kit picked up her fan and said, toward Belle's younger sister, "This means I accept."

"Oh!" Grace picked up a fan of fancy cut paper with a shiny black stock. "Like this?"

"No!" protested both Kit and Belle in unison, but Grace had already dropped it. The crack, when the fan hit the floor, was resounding.

Grace pressed her hand to her mouth. "Oh."

"It was glass, dear heart," explained Belle gamely, kneeling to pick up the remains. "We should have told you."

"No harm done," agreed Kit. "I'm sure I'll manage another visit to India—soon."

But I'm not *clumsy,* Grace told herself, determined. *I'm* not.

"Let us try a different signal." Belle picked up a fan that looked to be made of cedar and silk, and pressed it into Grace's now-empty hand. "If you wish to tell Mr. James that he has won your love—"

"But I hardly know him!"

Her sister smiled, beautiful as ever in her patience. "We are thinking positively, Grace. If you wish to tell him he has won your love, you use the fan to indicate your heart, like so."

Belle demonstrated with a feathered fan of the kind Grace didn't dare touch, ever since a certain disaster with white feathers and hungry cats.

Grace tapped her own chest with her fan.

"Something like that," said Belle. "But if you want to accuse him of being cruel, you do this."

Looking at Kit, the older sister deliberately opened and then shut her fan with a snap.

"I do hope, darling, that you were merely demonstrating," he laughed. "Or should I be concerned?"

Belle used her fan to indicate her heart, and Kit's loving smile made Grace want to cry. But she had a lesson to learn, so she said, "To tell him he's being cruel?"

Both Belle and Kit looked back to her, distracted from each other. "Yes," said Belle.

"But if he's being cruel, should I not just . . . slap him?"

Now the older couple exchanged worried looks.

"You see, Grace," said Kit, "you are more pretending that he has been cruel. In a rather . . . social way. If perhaps he is not paying enough attention, or has looked at another woman, or says something you dislike."

"That kind of cruel," agreed Belle. "Not as if he, oh . . . kicked you."

Grace was unsure she would call someone's lack of attention cruelty—especially not after what she'd learned at the previous week's lyceum about the plight of some children! But Belle and Kit were her teachers—until Comtesse Arabella awoke, anyhow. "Show me again?"

Belle opened the fan, then snapped it shut.

Grace tried it with hers, liking the dramatic snap. "Oh! I did it!"

"Except you must look at him, not the fan," corrected Belle. "Try it again. Pretend Kit is Mr. James."

Grace looked regally at Kit and tried the movement again, but her fan seemed stuck shut. "Oh, dear . . ."

Kit bent closer. "What is it?"

Then she managed to snap the fan open, hitting her future brother-in-law in the eye.

"Ow!" exclaimed Kit, clapping one gloved hand protectively to his face and backing quickly away.

"Oh, no!" exclaimed Belle, rushing to his side. "Are you all right?"

Horrified, Grace let the fan fall from her numb fingers, turned, and ran from the room. She ran through the house, through the kitchen, and out the back door. She would never manage to be graceful—*never*!

She would be Graceless Grace forever.

She had expected the cold to freeze her tears before she could cry them, but to her surprise, the air that washed across her, while cold, felt almost . . . gentle. She scented something different in it, something she usually welcomed with delight. . . .

Now it just brought more tears to join the muddy wetness of the still-snowy ground at her feet. Spring thaw. Winter was gradually ending. Soon the one person who seemed able to survive her—marginally—would leave forever. Jon would be gone, and the Founders Day ball would arrive, and she would be the only one of the Sullivan girls not to have used the blessing of the Three Graces to win the perfect man—or perhaps any man at all.

Then again, her fairy godmother had been upstairs asleep while she was abusing her sister's fiancé. What kind of fairy godmother was that?

Behind her, the door opened. Grace did not dare look, lest it turn out to be her mother, to scold her, or her father, to pretend nothing was wrong, or Belle, to report that Kit would have to wear an eye patch from now on.

Instead, Phronsy, the cook, draped a cape over Grace's shoulders. "The snow may be melting, Miss Grace, but it's still dreadful weather. You don't want to catch your death."

"But it won't be dreadful for long," said Grace listlessly. "The snow will go, and the creeks will flood, and the grass will come out, and the trees will leaf out, and there will be picnics and parties and fine clothes to ruin. . . . Oh, Phronsy, I don't want to stay in town anymore. I want to live up on the mountains, where things are simpler."

The cook put a comforting arm around her. "Things are only as complex or as simple as you make them."

Grace shook her head.

"Trust me," said Phronsy with a secret smile. "I'm older than I look."

But Grace knew better.

Jon breathed the sharp early spring air through the open window, a mere week later, and wished he could be happier about everything.

Everything like, oh, his getting well.

Or Grace being visited downstairs by the lauded Mr. Robert James.

None of your business, he told himself. Why shouldn't she have gentlemen callers?

But it annoyed him all the same.

His wrist felt better—good enough that he could probably use the crutches to attend family dinners again, if he dared. Considering how badly his last one had gone, he hesitated to risk lighting the Sullivan tinder a second time. Besides, he rather liked dining with little Gio. His leg felt increasingly better, too—the doctor said they could probably remove the plaster cast in another week. Although Jon knew that Colorado winters rarely made a single, graceful exit and that the snow could return well into the summer, the green mist of grass along the bottom of the mountains and the scent of life on the breeze finally promised the freedom and adventure for which he'd left Minnesota.

So why wasn't he happier?

"Did you know," asked Gio, sitting cross-legged on the bed with his nose in one of the promised books, "that there is a rock that looks like gold but is not?"

Not surprisingly, Gio had turned out to be an excellent reader. He'd only pretended ignorance so that Grace would come every night and read to them.

Jon felt bad about the deception but not bad enough to put a stop to Grace's nightly visits. "Yeah. I knew that."

Gio said, "It is called iron pyrite."

"Uh-huh."

"Fool's gold."

"Yeah." Jon imagined he could see the snow line actually creeping up the mountain range before his eyes, if he concentrated. That was how fast spring seemed to be getting a foothold. "I know."

"I think you need me to come along with you," decided Gio. "To tell the difference between iron pyrite and gold."

Jon closed his eyes. It was going to be hell to leave the kid behind. But he couldn't subject a child to the hard life of a miner. . . . Clearly, he had to find someplace else for the boy. Someplace that wouldn't crush Gio's determined spirit. Someplace that would encourage the boy's intelligence. Gio should be in school, not wandering the mountains.

Or hiding in his room, for that matter. "I can tell the difference."

"No, you cannot," insisted Gio. "You are a fool."

Very funny. Jon favored the kid with an overly dramatic sneer over his shoulder, so that Gio laughed. But Jon said, "You aren't coming with me. If that's why you've been reading up on mining. . . "

Gio raised his chin, as if not the least bit disturbed by that announcement. Lately, he'd taken to pretending that he didn't care what Jon did. "You are wrong. I am reading up on mining so that I can go mine for myself."

"You can't go mine for yourself."

"Who is going to stop me?"

Jon opened his mouth, then closed it to scowl back out the window. That was a good point. Who was going to stop the child from doing any number of foolish things once Jon left? The boy had already run away from an orphanage, crossed half the country on his own, followed a strange cook all the way from Denver, then hidden out in a millionaire's home for over three months.

If Gio stayed where it was safe, clearly he had to do it of his own accord. Jon suspected even Phronsy's cooking wasn't enough to keep the kid in town. So he said, "You can't go mine for yourself because you can't leave Grace behind."

Gio's dark eyes narrowed with immediate suspicion. "Why should it matter to Miss Grace if I am here or not?"

"Because she might be a little, uh, put out when I leave." *Or she might barely notice.* Jon still hadn't heard any activity far below from the front door. How long was that James fellow going to loiter around the Sullivan parlor, anyway?

"Then don't leave."

"I can't stay permanently," Jon said. "The Sullivans might notice me wandering around once I'm all healed up."

"Then break something else." Gio grinned. "Miss Grace will help, yes?"

Jon pointed a warning at the boy. "The last two times weren't Grace's fault, either. Don't even joke about that. I mean it."

Gio lifted the book to his nose again. "I came west for a reason, too. I am going to be rich, like Mr. Sullivan, except that I shall be happy about it."

Damn it, what was going on down there? "Is that man never going to leave?"

"What man?" As if Gio didn't know everything that went on in this house.

"Robert James." Funny how the name came out almost like a snarl. "'Of the Denver Jameses.'"

Gio just shrugged. "You are feeling so much better, you find out."

Suddenly, that seemed like the perfect idea.

Jon grabbed his crutches and swung out the door of his room, disoriented by the sense of returned freedom. When he reached the landing, he transferred both crutches to one hand and used the banister with his other.

He would go downstairs and take a look at this Mr. Robert James. If the man looked like he would ever hurt Grace, Jon could clobber him with a crutch. But if he didn't . . .

Well, wouldn't it help him to leave to know that Grace would not be alone?

One flight of stairs down, two to go.

The lower Jon descended, the more sense it made. It occurred to him that he was in his shirt-sleeves, as opposed to how well this James fellow likely dressed, but he wasn't going back up for his one good suit jacket now. If that James person acted like a snob about it . . .

His grip on the crutches tightened.

By the time he reached the first floor and the entryway to the parlor, Jon wasn't sure which he wanted more: to see that Grace was madly in love with this new suitor of hers or to see her cringing helplessly from him like the heroine in a good melodrama.

So that Jon could put the crutches to good use.

He slowed his swinging step, though, confused, when the scene before him showed neither extreme.

The three Sullivan girls sat primly on a settee, pretty as a picture in gowns that had a special brightness to them, probably in honor of spring's arrival. Grace, in particular, had never looked prettier despite the frills on her apple green gown; her red hair all but glowed. Their mother and that Arabella woman stood in the corner as proper chaperons. Accordingly, the three men in the room were also on their feet: Kit Stanhope, his eye bruised as if from a prize fight, but otherwise whole; Will Barclay, bending over Charisma to murmur something to her . . .

And Robert James of the Denver Jameses.

The man stood comfortably beside Grace, holding a cup of tea, smiling a perfectly friendly smile. He was not as tall as Jon—not even as tall as Stanhope or Barclay—but neither was he short, and the cut of his coat emphasized a surprisingly fit figure for a man who didn't have to work.

He didn't appear to be the sort who would lean toward mustache twirling or scheming evil plots.

So, thought Jon, *be happy for her. Problem solved.*

Except that Grace did not look happy for herself. She was as pretty as one of her mother's porcelain figurines, with her penny-bright hair carefully drawn back and her skin fresh as a pail of milk, and her precious face, and her large eyes . . .

But she seemed as stiff as a ceramic figurine, too.

Comtesse Arabella noticed Jon first. At least, he figured that was why she made the strange hissing noise. The others looked up quickly. Mrs. Sullivan flushed with displeasure.

Charisma, however, stepped right into the void left by their chaperons. "Mr. Erikson. How pleasant to see you downstairs once more. Of course you know Misters Barclay and Stanhope."

"Erikson," greeted Patrick Sullivan's future sons-in-law.

"This," continued Charisma, "is Mr. Robert James. Mr. James, Jon Erikson's family has a long history with my father; he has been staying with us since injuring his leg earlier this year."

James placed his teacup on the doilied table beside Grace and came forward, offering his hand. "Erikson. Good to meet you."

They shook firmly but without any competitive posturing. So much for the man being a snob. If Robert James disliked being forced to socialize with a fellow in his shirtsleeves, he had better manners than to show it.

Feeling distinctly outclassed as well as under-dressed, Jon just said, "Hello. I, uh . . . I didn't mean to interrupt. I'm just, uh, stretching my legs."

"Doing pretty well at it, too," said Barclay, who had apparently healed up from his dancing injury just fine. "You'll be free of that cast soon, no doubt."

Jon nodded—and glanced toward Grace. "Yeah," he agreed, his throat tight. "I'll be moving on any day now."

When Grace lifted her gaze to his, it was with such longing, he almost stumbled back. Couldn't she see that he was just a drifter, with neither the money nor the class to have any kind of future with her? She wasn't going to get a much better illustration of how much more articulate and mannered and fashionable the Jameses and Stanhopes and Barclays of the world were in contrast to this burly, simple son of a Norwegian immigrant.

And yet the need in her gaze made Jon feel as if the earth were sliding out from underneath him . . . and he couldn't tell whether he was more frightened or excited by the sensation.

Not until he noticed Bridget Mary Sullivan glaring at him with eyes of sheer rage.

Chapter Fourteen

Now Jon did take a step back, awkward or not. "I should leave you folks to your, er . . . your socializing."

"Thank you for stopping by, Mr. Erikson." But Mrs. Sullivan's words in no way matched her expression. Something had moved her from mere dislike of Jon to something that resembled hatred—but what?

"Good to meet you," said James.

It was Grace who said, "Wait—"

But as she reached out as if to stop him, her sleeve somehow caught in the doily beside her, and the next thing anyone knew, the abandoned teacup seemed to leap off the side table, then splashed across the front of Robert James's trousers, and bounced to the floor.

Where it shattered.

Grace's eyes widened, and she pressed a hand to her mouth. Jon readjusted his crutches to go to her side, Mrs. Sullivan be damned.

But James got there first. "Miss Grace, I am so very sorry. How could I have been so careless as to leave that cup there?"

Grace looked up at her gentleman caller, her astonishment almost as palpable as her obvious need for the reassurance.

"Please forgive me," continued Robert James, pulling a neatly folded handkerchief from his pocket and pressing it onto a tiny spill of tea on Grace's hand, ignoring his own embarrassingly wet trousers. "Please say you'll still accompany me to the Founder's Day ball next week?"

Mrs. Sullivan and Comtesse Arabella exchanged glances of triumph. Belle's and Charisma's expressions looked more delighted, and even Stanhope and Barclay seemed to approve. And why not?

The man was upright. Damn it. Jon couldn't have handled the situation better himself.

So he simply backed out of the parlor, crutches and all, while nobody was noticing.

Grace spent a great deal of her week in the kitchen, despite her mother's protests.

"Men like Robert James can afford cooks," Mama stated firmly when Phronsy announced at dinner that Grace had made their dessert.

Grace tried not to notice how dubiously Belle and Charisma eyed the cake, as if afraid that its prettily frosted exterior must hide some kind of gaffe in the ingredients. They did, after all, have a basis for suspicion. She was still amazed that she'd hardly dropped, spilled, broken, or set fire to anything.

"As for me," said Da heartily, "I've been missing the taste of home baking. Thank you, Gracie."

Mama sat back in her dinner chair. "Missed

home baking? And where is it you think Cook does her work—Dublin?"

Da cut a piece of the cake. "You know my meaning, Bridey."

"Sure and I don't, Mr. Sullivan. But if you're referring to the time I earned our living making bread for an entire mining camp, it's because you weren't the one doing the baking! I kneaded dough until my hands cramped—"

Comtesse Arabella cleared her throat, looking embarrassed by such a low-class anecdote.

Mama looked embarrassed,too. "Gracie need never know that kind of hardship, is all I'm saying."

Grace said, "But I *like* baking."

"The weather or your health, Grace," corrected Comtesse Arabella, who had a very limited view of proper conversational topics.

Da said, "My name is Paddy." But for once he said it low and quiet, almost sad. The tired edge to his tone unsettled Grace worse than his shouts ever had.

Before she could worry too much about that, Da said, "So you like this Robert James fellow, do you, Grace? It's not just your mother's interference has you going to this ball?"

Suddenly, everyone seemed to be looking at Grace with extra interest, and it made her nervous. She knocked over her water glass—which Phronsy quickly righted—before she said, "Of course I like him, Da. He's a very nice man."

Which was true. He'd asked to call on her, despite how distracted she'd been at the lyceum. When he did call on her, he'd asked to escort her to the Founder's Day ball, apparently of his own volition. He did not seem to mind terribly when she spilled or dropped things on him, or when she stepped or fell on him; in fact, he handled it almost as smoothly as Jon. In fact, Robert seemed to think Grace's lack of coordination was cute.

What was there not to like?

And yet Grace didn't miss Belle and Charisma exchanging concerned looks at her less-than-enthusiastic answer.

"*Don't* you want to go to the ball with Mr. James?" demanded Charisma the moment the older girls got Grace alone in Belle's room.

"Of course I do." But Grace looked at her hands as she spoke. "I said yes, didn't I?"

"Well . . . yes," hedged Belle, doubtful. "But . . ."

"You didn't seem particularly enthusiastic about it," finished Charisma, forthright as ever. "You certainly don't seem to be, well . . . in love."

I've barely met the man on a handful of occasions, Grace thought. But the promise of what Charisma said took precedence. "Tell me," she pleaded. "Tell me what being in love seems like."

Her sisters exchanged uncertain glances.

"It's as Mama always says," Belle answered.

"That it's as easy to fall in love with a rich man as a poor one?"

Belle narrowed her eyes chidingly. "That you know it when you feel it."

Grace flopped back on Belle's bed. "You mean it's a secret."

"I mean no such thing."

Grace sat up again. "But it is! You and Charisma

have kept secrets ever since you fell in love with Kit and Will. How am I supposed to learn if nobody tells me anything?"

"If we've kept secrets, dear," demurred Belle, "it has been about private matters."

Something so private that it could only be shared with one sister and not the other? Perhaps Grace's expression reflected her dismay, because Charisma chimed in.

"Our behavior has not always been as proper as Mama would like you to believe."

Belle gasped slightly to hear it said flat out.

Grace stared at her second sister, slowly piecing together what that meant. Then she looked at Belle, then back to Charisma.

Then her mouth widened. "You *crossed invisible lines?*"

Belle said, "I believe the details are our own affair."

Charisma snorted, and Belle shot her a deadly look.

"Oh," said Grace, still amazed. She'd thought her older sisters were near perfect, yet they'd courted scandal in ways they could not even tell her! Oh, she doubted they'd *completely* lost their honor. They *were* her sisters, after all, and their fiancés were true gentlemen.

That mysterious area between complete propriety and ruin must hold more possibilities than Grace had ever considered. "Oh, my."

"None of this resolves our original concern," Belle forged on. "You don't seem to be as enamored of Mr. James as our mother would like."

"You mean I don't want to kiss him?" Or any of

those other wonderful, secret, mysterious-area things her sisters wouldn't tell her?

Belle said, "It is not just about wanting to kiss, Grace."

At the same time, Charisma said, "Yes."

Grace shrugged—a movement that Comtesse Arabella, were she there, would surely protest. "Did you want to kiss Will from the start, Charisma? Belle, you wanted to take revenge on Kit when you first began courting with him. Surely you were not in love right off."

"Perhaps not *right* off." But Belle still looked uncomfortable.

Suddenly, Grace understood. She had not wanted to kiss Jon right off, either, but she'd certainly enjoyed looking into his summertime blue eyes. He'd seemed somehow different, more important than any other man, and not just because he'd saved her life.

He still felt different. Special.

Jon.

But why couldn't he be someone of whom her family might approve? Unfortunately for Grace's dilemma, both Belle and Charisma had fallen for men their parents adored. She had no precedent by which to balance her priorities.

Grace tried a different way of pressing her next question, a way that she hoped would not betray her own secret. "If I do not find a match with Mr. James, I might yet with someone else wonderful, mightn't I?"

Belle sat beside her to give her a quick hug. "Of course you shall."

"But I bet you and Mr. James will hit it off at the

Founder's Day ball," added Charisma. "It's too like
Belle's and my own courtships, after all. Madame
Aglaia's beautiful dresses helped Belle win Kit. The
widow Poppadopolous helped me better understand Will and the role of a politician's wife. Since
Comtesse Arabella arrived, she has helped you
catch the eye of Robert James. . . ."

"True." Belle stroked back Grace's hair. "It seems
as if, after our wish to the Three Graces, anything is
possible."

Anything? Even me loving a miner?

Grace couldn't quite bring herself to ask that—
or to say that for a fairy godmother, the *comtesse* had
yet to impress her in any way good.

She'd learned more from Phronsy and her baking.

"I suppose we'll see," she said.

Jon was ready to leave. Really, he was.

As soon as he convinced Grace to find a home
for Gio.

Preferably her own.

He stood by the open window, watching her on
the bed. She'd been reading to the boy but had
been diverted to teaching him mining camp songs
she remembered from her childhood: "The Days of
'49" and "Sweet Betsy from Pike." She had even
whistled a few bars of each, a skill Gio could not yet
duplicate, but when the kid begged her to continue, she blushed, shook her head, and insisted it
wasn't ladylike.

Watching her lips, pursed or otherwise, Jon decided he really preferred her not being ladylike.

More important, though, he felt certain she and Gio were meant for each other.

In a mother-child relationship, of course.

She softly sang, "Oh, I miss the boys and all the noise, and the gold that once was mine." But her gaze slid up toward Jon's, her eyes especially bright. "In the days of old, the days of gold, the days of 'forty-nine . . ."

He felt such a sharp pang in his chest that he had to look out the window. She'd been doing that for three days now, slanting looks at him, smiling for no reason, seeming to start to say something, then not.

He was afraid of what she might want to say—and afraid of what she might not. Either she was sweet on him, Jon Erikson, and wanted to say so—which, he had to remind his speeding heartbeat, would be a *bad* thing—or she was sweet on that Robert James fellow and couldn't stop thinking about him even when she was with Jon and Gio.

Good thing, thought Jon sternly, staring out at the mix of green and brown peeking through the remains of the previous night's snow. *That would be the good thing. Really.*

His heartbeat did not agree.

He sneaked a glance back toward the bed, relieved that Grace had bent her auburn head back over the book, continuing her recitation upon the differing qualities of ore. She had such beautiful, fiery hair, and such a graceful posture. Her lashes seemed so long in profile . . .

Gio's dark gaze was the one that caught Jon this time. The little boy's eyebrows came up, curious.

Jon narrowed his eyes in warning.

Suddenly, Gio coughed, interrupting the reading. He put his hand to his mouth and coughed harder.

Grace put down the book and rubbed his back, immediately concerned. "Are you all right? Have you caught cold?"

Gio shook his head quickly, curls bouncing. "I think I need milk," he suggested, giving Grace the ten-cent treatment with his big, dark eyes. *The little faker.* "Milk, and more of those wonderful cookies you made, Miss Grace."

Jon said, "You don't need any milk and cookies."

Gio ignored him completely. "Please, Miss Grace, will you excuse me?"

Grace gave the boy a quick hug. "Of course you're excused!"

Now the boy glanced toward Jon—with triumph. "I will be right back," he said, clambering off the bed. "Hold my place, please."

And before Jon could protest, they'd been left alone.

Uff da. Jon had resolved not to be alone with Grace again since his visit to the parlor. Not only was he worried about Bridey Sullivan's increased animosity toward him, he wasn't sure he could keep from interfering in what would be a far better future for Grace as one of the Denver Jameses.

Or for him, as Fortune's companion and Destiny's damned beau.

All he had to do before escaping, he reminded himself, was secure Gio's own future.

"So," he said. "Are you excited about the big ball coming up?"

Grace said, "I suppose."

"That James fellow seems pretty nice."

Now Grace cocked her head. "I suppose."

"Do you know if he likes children?" asked Jon.

But at the same time, Grace said, "I'm rather worried, actually." Then she blinked, catching the end of his question. "What?"

Pursue his own argument, or see why she was worried? Pursue his own argument, or . . .

Damn.

"Why are you worried?" asked Jon, a sinking sensation in his chest.

Grace got off the bed—which had to be a good thing—and stood beside it. "I haven't practiced dancing since that last time. You know, when I nearly lamed poor Will."

"I told you that wasn't your fault."

"And since you showed me how wonderful dancing could be." She looked up at him, the yearning in her gaze unmistakable. "Would you mind giving me another lesson?"

Jon stared at her, sensing Fortune and Destiny turning up their noses at him as he did. Good riddance to them. There was nothing more important than Grace Sullivan at this moment. "Yes," he said, limping across the room to her without the help of crutches. He took her soft hands in his, breathed the scent of flour and vanilla off her fiery hair, lost himself in the depths of her eyes, her longing. "Yes, I'd be glad to."

But when Grace wrapped her arms around his waist, it wasn't to dance. When he slid his hand behind her back to pull her close, he was holding on to her for a completely different purpose. Whether he was drawing her nearer or she was leaning into him of her own volition, he would never guess. What mattered was that she rose onto her toes as he bent to her and touched her lips with his . . .

And found all the future he could possibly want.

Grace . . .

He did not know how to tell her, how to ask her, beyond their kisses. What did he have to offer compared to her rich society beaux, beyond this? But he sensed without asking that she did no care, and he knew he could no longer be the strong one.

When they could breathe again, speak again, that would be soon enough for words, perhaps even for plans. But for now . . .

He'd never known a completion so certain as holding Grace Sullivan in his arms. Everything seemed possible.

Until the door flew open, revealing her parents.

Chapter Fifteen

One moment, Grace had found that heaven was summertime blue. The next, she'd been tossed out. Even as she startled at the banging door, Jon had swept her protectively behind him . . .

But not before she saw her parents' shocked faces.

"I knew it!" exclaimed Mama. "I knew from the way she looked at him."

"I never would have believed it," Da all but whispered. "Not my little Gracie . . ."

Jon said, "It's my doing, sir. Not hers."

"Damned right it is!" Da bellowed.

That's when Grace had to lean out from behind Jon, despite how ill she felt to see her parents so hurt. Truth was truth. "It was my doing, too."

"Be quiet," murmured Jon, trying to push her back into hiding.

"No!"

"Do you truly want to know whose doing this is, Patrick Sullivan?" demanded Mama. "It's yours, for bringing that ruffian into our home in the first place!"

Oh, no! Bad enough to be disgraced, but for

Mama to blame it on Da . . . "It isn't!" Grace insisted.

Da said, "Is that what you're thinking, Bridey? And on whose shoulders does the blame fall for Charisma and Belle?"

Jon glanced over his shoulder at Grace, eyes bright with curiosity. Grace wished she knew more of the story herself. She shrugged.

"At least Charisma and Belle had high-class beaux," Mama said. "At least Charisma and Belle caught themselves fine husbands. This man is a . . . a . . ."

"A complete gentleman!" Grace insisted, pushing past Jon's hip far enough to face her parents on her own. "Jon has been nothing but a gentleman from the start."

Neither of the elder Sullivans looked convinced. It occurred to Grace that to some extent, she'd just lied.

"Except for when he kisses me," she admitted—and shrank back from her father's clear fury.

"Not the help I need," murmured Jon, drawing her behind him again. She let him, in part because she certainly wasn't doing much good, and in part . . .

In part because she couldn't help but think everything could still work out, if only she just kept close to Jon.

"So you admit it, then?" demanded Da, which confused her. Of course she admitted to kissing Jon! Then he said, "You admit to prostituting our girls in your godforsaken pursuit of social standing?"

He was talking not to Grace but to his wife.

The sound of a slap was unmistakable.

Then Da said nothing.

Grace did not want to look. She didn't.

But she had to.

Mama still had her hand up. Da's cheek bloomed with the impact of her blow. Both of them were staring at each other in horror, as if they didn't know each other, as if forgetting to even breathe.

Grace had never seen her parents look so very . . . lost.

It was Mama who spoke first. "Get out of my home."

DA?

Mama turned to Jon. "Get out of my home, you Norwegian pig." Her voice increased in volume and brogue with every word. "Get away from my daughter. Get away from my town. I never wanted you here, and damned I'll be if I'll allow you to besmirch our family one minute more! Do you understand me, boyo? *Do you?*"

Jon said, "Yes, ma'am." Grace wished she could see his expression.

Da, to her horror, still said nothing.

"No," Grace said again, to everyone. "You don't understand—"

A scuffle in the hallway interrupted her. Someone—it sounded like Comtesse Arabella—screeched. Then a black-haired blur whooshed by.

Except Da caught the blur, little Gio, before he made his escape. "And what's this?"

Gio struggled, wriggled, and kicked. But Da kept a solid hold on him.

"I caught this urchin spying on you!" announced

the *comtesse*, huffing into the doorway, flapping her hand. "He *bit* me!"

"Put him down," said Jon, rocking slightly forward as if unsure whether to go to Gio or stay in front of Grace.

"Jesus, Mary, and Joseph," exclaimed Mama. "Is that child *Italian*? In *our* house?"

Jon took a step and said, more firmly, "You're scaring him, Mr. Sullivan. *Put him down.*"

"Is this one yours, then?" demanded Da, all but staggering back at this latest surprise. Grace drew breath to explain Gio's complicated history even as the child turned bright eyes pleadingly toward Jon. Sometimes it was easy to forget how little Gio was, what with his feisty ways, but he really was young. And Da was used to dealing with full-grown miners.

"Da," Grace protested.

But Jon strode forward and lifted Gio from Da's grasp. "Yeah," he said. "He's mine."

Gio wrapped his skinny arms around Jon's neck and hid his face in Jon's chest. Grace's eyes stung as she watched Jon raise a single large, protective hand to the boy's back. She'd never seen a pairing that felt more right.

Except . . .

Except she wasn't part of it. In going to Gio, Jon had left her behind. If she went to him, would he include her in his embrace with the child? Was that all it would take to be included?

And yet, at what cost?

"Quiet," commanded Da, over Mama and Comtesse Arabella's exclamations. "*Quiet*, I say! I'll get to the bottom of this, if you two women will stop yapping like excited lapdogs."

"Call me a dog again, Paddy Sullivan," warned Mama, "and I'll blacken your eye!"

From the hallway, Grace heard her sisters approaching. "Whatever is going on?" demanded Belle. "We could hear the shouting from the first floor!"

Comtesse Arabella sidled into the room and took Grace's arm. "Come, Grace. You mustn't get too close to the child. He might have vermin."

For maybe the first time, Grace saw Jon's eyes narrow in true anger. He was clearly above being rude to a lady, but he just as clearly wished he weren't.

Luckily, Grace didn't have to be gentlemanly about anything. "Shut up," she told the *comtesse*.

She'd never realized how powerful simple rudeness could be. The *comtesse did* shut up. So did Da, and Mama, and Belle, and Charisma. Gio turned his face from Jon's chest to smile wetly at her.

Jon winked his approval, and she loved him.

But it was a temporary lull. Suddenly everyone—everyone except Jon and Gio—began shouting at Grace for being rude. Worse, Comtesse Arabella pulled on Grace's arm, clearly ready to manhandle her out of the room and away from the suspect immigrants if necessary. Maybe Arabella *was* Grace's fairy godmother, sent by the Three Graces monument and her sisters' wish, but . . .

Grace pulled back. Wish or not, she wasn't doing anything else that felt wrong.

"You see what the wrong kind of company has done to her!" exclaimed Mama.

"You're already in enough trouble, Gracie," warned Da, "behaving like that!"

"It wasn't Grace's fault," insisted Jon.

Now Arabella yanked. It hurt.

"Behaving like what?" asked Charisma, intrigued. "*What* wasn't Grace's fault?"

"Grace," protested Belle, clearly distraught, "what has gotten into you?"

"Gio and I will go," said Jon, as if to pacify everyone.

That was *not* what Grace wanted to hear. She set her feet and yanked back, hard. When her arm slipped free of the *comtesse*'s tight-fingered grip, both of them stumbled back. Grace rolled onto Jon's bed, her skirts flying every which way, which only made Mama shout more loudly.

Arabella flew back against the armoire where Grace and Gio had once hidden. Her body made a solid thud with the impact. The wardrobe rocked. Sitting up, Grace saw Belle cover her mouth to catch back a scream as, for a moment, it looked as if the tall dresser might fall on their guest. Instead, the armoire righted itself.

But only after spilling a hail of silverware onto Comtesse Arabella's head.

As soon as he saw the silver spoons raining down onto the shrieking noblewoman's head, Jon understood what had happened.

The way Gio hid his face again, with a muffled *"Uff da,"* only confirmed it.

He'd been leaving anyway, of course. He never should have stayed so long. But suddenly, the issue wasn't so much leaving gracefully as leaving without the involvement of lawmen or violence. Yet instead of eyeing the exit, Jon found himself watching Grace.

And not just because her tumble onto the bed revealed an attractive length of green-stockinged legs or pulled her curly mass of auburn hair loose. He *was* leaving now, as he'd always meant to. He was taking Gio with him, which he hadn't planned but which, with the guilt-ridden child heavy in his arms, felt surprisingly right all the same.

But what about Grace?

She pushed a tangle of hair off her face, leaning forward to look at the scattering of silverware on the floor. She looked, wide-eyed, up at Jon.

He considered trying to grin it away with aw-shucks humor—*I can explain that*—or pretending to be shocked—*What are those doing there?*

Then Patrick Sullivan said, "You heard my wife, Erikson. Take your Italian bastard and get the hell out of Colorado Springs."

And Jon said, "*Gladly.* Grace?"

Slowly she sat up in the bed, drawing her legs under her, looking from one of her loved ones to another—and then to Jon. Was he a loved one, too, or had he just imagined it? "Da," she protested, and her voice quavered. "You don't—"

"Not another word from you," Sullivan warned. "*Now,* Erikson!"

"Grace," repeated Jon, and Sullivan took a threatening step toward him. Maybe Jon *could* take the older man. Then again, Jon still had a hurt leg, a sore wrist, and an armful of Gio.

Who was shivering.

Clearly, Grace was torn. That had to mean she

was *considering* going with him. But just as clearly, she wasn't sure.

And this was far too much to ask of her, if she wasn't sure.

"Take care, Grace," said Jon. He shouldered the pack he'd come with, glanced at the crutches Sullivan had given him, then limped awkwardly out without them.

Between his plaster cast, Gio, and the pack, the going was even more awkward than the tense situation warranted. But nothing would persuade him to accept a red cent from the man who'd housed and fed him for all these weeks and who now truly believed Jon had robbed him.

The Sullivan women—Belle, Charisma, and their mother—stepped back to make room for Jon. Sullivan watched him through narrow eyes, as if daring Jon even to pause, which Jon did not.

Behind him, he heard the *comtesse* say, "You should search his bag, Mr. Sullivan! Heaven only knows what he—"

Then he heard all three Sullivan girls say, "Shut up!"

It was almost enough to make him smile as he hobbled slowly down the too-wide, too-grand staircase that had kept him imprisoned in grandeur for so long. Almost.

But since he was leaving Grace behind, Jon wasn't sure *anything* could make him smile again.

"Perhaps Comtesse Arabella wasn't sent by the Three Graces after all," said Belle.

The three girls were seated about Belle's bedchamber, trying to ignore the shouts that rang through the mansion. At least, Belle and Charisma were trying to ignore them. Grace hardly noticed.

The pain of hearing her parents berate each other felt mild compared to the aching confusion she felt over Jon's departure. He'd said her name twice. Was he asking her to go with him? Even if he *had* been asking, could she have gone? Just like that?

How could she leave her family in this kind of turmoil?

"She certainly seems far less helpful than Aglaia," continued Belle.

"Or the widow Poppadopoulos," agreed Charisma. "But wishes and Greek mythology aside, *I* want to know what Grace was doing in Jon Erikson's room."

When Grace remembered—the scent of him, the strength of him, the adoration and acceptance in his kisses—she felt a delicious calm steal over her . . . until she remembered that he was gone. He'd gone, and she hadn't gone with him.

Then everything just hurt worse.

She didn't care what her sisters thought of her anymore. She wasn't sure she cared about anything. "I was kissing him."

She felt rebellious saying it flat out like that. She didn't care about that, either.

But despite her resolve not to care, the way Belle and Charisma reacted intrigued her. They didn't gasp in horror, or recoil from her, or immediately chide her.

Instead, they glanced at each other, then back at Grace—with complete understanding.

Belle took Grace's hand in hers and gently asked, "Do you love him, Gracie?"

Grace nodded. "I know Mama always says it's as easy to love a rich man as a poor one, but I don't care. I love Jon. And now . . ."

Her eyes burned with unshed tears. Now her family thought the worst of him, thought him a thief and the father of an illegitimate immigrant child.

Now he was gone.

"Phooey," said Charisma, lifting her chin. "As if we can choose whom to love from the pages of the Montgomery Ward catalogue! I didn't expect to fall in love with Will the way I did."

Belle nodded. "I thought I *hated* Kit."

They still weren't chiding Grace. Grace said, "Jon didn't steal that silver. I suppose Gio did, but he didn't *do* anything with it."

"No harm done," agreed Charisma loyally.

Grace looked from one sister to the other. "You don't think I'm a fool for believing in Jon? For falling in love with him?"

Belle said, "I believed in Kit when hardly anybody else did, and he certainly hasn't disappointed me."

"You know him better than we do," said Charisma, with only a little reproach in her voice over Grace's secrecy.

From downstairs the shouting continued. Occasionally, something shattered against a wall.

Grace could hardly believe that her sisters were taking this so very well. "Then . . . you don't think I'm a floozy?"

Again Belle and Charisma exchanged secret glances. But this time, instead of retreating into mysterious silence, Belle said, "We should probably tell you something about our own courtships, Grace . . ."

When Euphrosyne arrived back at Mount Olympus, she found her sisters pacing.

"How could he leave like that?" demanded Thalia.

"Why did she not go with him?" demanded Aglaia.

Exhausted by the day, and not just from her chores in the kitchen, Euphrosyne sank into a cloud and closed her eyes. "He left because he is Jon," she said. "Because it is what he has meant to do all along. He values his freedom. And she stayed because she is Grace, and her family is what she has valued all along, and she values their opinions." She opened her eyes.

Thalia stopped pacing and scowled at her. "A less than stellar match, then!"

"Perhaps."

Aglaia asked, "So what do you intend to do about it?"

Euphrosyne glanced sadly toward the bowl of water in which the Graces had been looking and listening in on the Sullivans' lives since the request they'd received in the Garden of the Gods.

"We wait," she said.

Chapter Sixteen

By breakfast the next morning, Grace was still reeling from what her sisters had revealed about themselves and their fiancés. For one thing, it was easier to focus on that than the fact that Jon had left.

Had left her behind.

For another, it was a truly shocking revelation. The couples had already, as Charisma put it, "more than kissed."

And neither sister seemed repentant.

At first, as she sat down to the breakfast table, Grace was unsure whether she could even look at Belle or Charisma without blushing.

Of course, not looking proved impossible. She sneaked a peek at Belle and felt some relief to see that her oldest sister was just, well, *Belle*. Tall and fair and no-nonsense. Charisma, when Grace peeked at her, looked as energetic and determined as ever, even if her determination focused on the food before her.

Grace still wasn't quite sure how to feel about the fact that her beloved, respected sisters had flouted society's conventions to such an extent. She certainly had no right to judge them—they'd had their own consequences to deal with and their own decisions to make. Goodness, Grace might gladly have crossed invisible lines with Jon, given the opportunity!

Her chest hurt, so she tried not to think of Jon.

Still, because of him she wasn't as embarrassed as she'd thought she might be. She could no more picture Belle or Charisma giving themselves up to passion than she could imagine their parents . . . !

It was unimaginable.

Especially when Mama all but stumbled into the dining room, red-eyed and worn. Normally, she dressed up for breakfast, a fact that their father continually teased her about. But this morning she wore a simple wrapper and did not appear to have combed her hair.

"Mama?" asked Charisma when Belle and Grace sat in stunned silence. Only Phronsy, in the midst of serving individual portions of ham, did not stare—and likely she was ignoring her mistress's dishabille on purpose. "Are you feeling all right?"

Mama said nothing at first. She only sank, straight-backed and tight-lipped, into her chair.

That was when Grace noticed that their father hadn't arrived yet. Da was often late for dinner, a meal whose formality he hated. But breakfast . . .

The early bird catches the worm, Da always said.

No. Oh, no!

"Where's Da?" Grace's voice came out higher than she'd meant, and she immediately regretted her question with a sick feeling deep inside. She did not want to know the answer.

Too late.

"I have asked your father to move out," said

Mama, only the faintest edge betraying her attempt at firmness. "He has complied."

What?

For a long moment, nobody spoke. Nobody even moved—not even Phronsy, who looked particularly sympathetic from her corner by the sideboard. Then Charisma—of course Charisma—demanded, *"Why?"*

"That matter is between your father and myself," said Mama.

The Sullivan sisters exchanged horrified glances. Then Grace, though she dreaded this answer, too, asked, "Was it because of Jon and me?"

"Please do not speak so familiarly about that kind of man," snapped Mama.

That kind of man? But Mama was clearly upset— Grace could not remember her mother ever taking so little care of her appearance, not even when they were a normal mining family in Leadville. So she tried again. "Was it because of Mr. Erikson and me?"

"Grace!" Mama took a deep, angry breath. "I misspoke. Do not speak of that man at all."

"But if he's why you made Da move out—"

"And you will stop using that vulgar name for your father," continued Mama. "If you must, call him 'Papa,' as your sisters do. 'Father' would be better, though. And it is none of your business why your father moved out."

Belle said, "Perhaps we should retire upstairs, Grace."

But Grace thought about Jon, and little Gio, and how content she'd felt in their company. She'd been more at ease with them than she'd felt for a long time, perhaps ever since her older sisters' engagement. It was not that she begrudged Belle or Charisma a moment of their hard-won happiness. But they had moved on, become their best possible selves, and she'd felt left behind.

Until Jon.

"No," she said.

Mama closed her eyes and raised a hand to her forehead. "I do not understand why you persist in being so contrary all of a sudden, young lady, but you will desist. The Founder's Day ball is day after tomorrow, and Comtesse Arabella is very close to giving you up as a lost cause—"

"Mother!" protested Charisma.

But Grace stood. "Good! I hope she does give me up, because I'm giving *her* up. I don't want to be graceful, if it makes me anything like her."

"Grace," warned Belle.

Mama said, "Some things, Grace, are worth a little difficulty."

"But just because they're hard doesn't mean they're worthwhile. Comtesse Arabella said she was teaching me to be a lady, but all she did was teach me to behave like someone else. And she's rude herself. She said that Gio might have fleas!"

"Joe?" Mama winced in her confusion. "That nasty little Italian boy who helped steal our silver?"

"Gio's not nasty; he's amazingly bright. And nobody stole the silver. It's still here, isn't it? And it's not Da's fault that I kissed Jon; it was my decision, and I'm glad I did it! If not kissing someone as wonderful as Jon has anything to do with being graceful and ladylike, then I don't want it!"

Mama said, "Sit down before you break something, Grace."

And Grace, unable to bear more, stormed from the room to the one place she still felt truly safe in this house.

The kitchen.

She stood in the middle of the room, hands pressed to her mouth, and fought back tears. She'd been such an idiot, giving up her soul in bits and pieces in an attempt to keep her parents together, when it had been beyond her control from the start. She'd made so many mistakes. Perhaps if she'd told Da of her attraction to Jon from the start, her father might have approved, or even chaperoned them properly. Maybe if she'd questioned Comtesse Arabella's teachings right away, she would not have wasted so much time on such fleeting matters as posture and proper conversational topics while ignoring more important issues, like the fate of an orphaned boy.

That sunny afternoon in the Garden of the Gods when she and her sisters had made their wishes seemed so very long ago. Grace couldn't even remember exactly what she'd wished for—true love? True grace? All she could remember was feeling hurt and embarrassed—embarrassed of being someone Jon Erikson hadn't minded at all.

Belle had found beauty and love. Charisma had discovered charm and love.

Had Grace somehow wished wrong?

"I think," said Phronsy gently, "you may have mistaken the true meaning of grace."

Grace spun, startled that the cook seemed to read her mind—and her flying hand knocked a bowl from the kitchen table. Potatoes rolled and bounced away like an escaping herd. Was she really that hopeless?

Did it matter?

"Why . . . ?" tried Grace. But she started picking up potatoes, too.

"You said in the dining room that you did not wish to be graceful," clarified Phronsy, which relieved Grace. Of *course* Phronsy had simply overheard. "Perhaps you should rethink what it means to be graceful."

"You mean, other than refinement? And not breaking things?"

Phronsy took the potatoes Grace handed up from the floor. "Other than that."

But she was so terribly clumsy—that had always been her worst fault. Or . . . it had been since they'd moved to Colorado Springs. What else could Grace want more than refinement?

Other than Jon, anyway?

"What else can *grace* mean?" prompted Phronsy.

Grace handed her the last of the potatoes and tried: "Being closer to God?"

When the cook smiled mysteriously, she looked downright beautiful. In a dark, ageless way. "That, too. But what else?"

Grace shook her head, unsure it mattered. What mattered was that every important man in her life had gone, and she'd done nothing to stop them.

"Your name comes from the French, which comes from Latin," explained Phronsy. "*Gratus*. It means something dear, or beloved. Or agreeable. Having grace, my dear, has far more to do with being of goodwill and kind heart than with moving effortlessly."

"I thought I was of goodwill." Grace rose far enough to sit on a kitchen chair, wiping her hands on her skirt. "And I *try* to be of kind heart."

Phronsy cocked her head, considering her. "Perhaps you would find it easier if you listened to your heart more often?"

The handbell from the dining room rang sharply—Mama summoning the help. Grace frowned, not liking the fact that her friend had to leave this conversation simply in order to serve food, but Phronsy lifted a platter of fried potatoes and left with it, not the least bit ruffled.

Graceful. In more ways than one.

"When do I not listen to my heart?" Grace asked softly, of nobody at all.

Then a solid knock sounded from the kitchen door, and her heart, the very one she'd just questioned, speeded in expectation. She knew whom she wanted to find at that door, unlikely though those hopes might be. If she were standing before the Three Graces' rock in the Garden of the Gods, she knew what she would wish.

The knock sounded again. Urgent. Defiant.

Since Phronsy was in the dining room, Grace went to the kitchen door and opened it.

And threw herself, full body and full heart, into Jon Erikson's waiting embrace.

Jon wasn't sure what he'd expected. Not this.

He wasn't arguing.

He folded Grace into his arms, dipping his head to rest his cheek on her head, to smell her hair. She was enough to soothe even his level of anxiety.

He'd hoped he could see her again despite having been tossed out of her family's home. Although she'd refused to come along, she hadn't exactly slammed the door behind him.

He knew her family would not want to see him again. He'd feared she would simply obey what her family asked of her.

But he wasn't about to doubt or protest her obvious welcome. "Hey, Gracie," he murmured, kissing her head. When she turned her face toward his, he was happy to move the kiss to her mouth. . . .

God, yes . . .

He hadn't meant to risk returning to the mansion so soon, but clearly he'd made the right choice. What had brought him here tightened his throat even as he drew back from this sweet, beloved woman.

"Gio's run away."

Grace's eyes widened, and she immediately protested, "He wouldn't!"

Jon appreciated her confidence in him, but that didn't change the truth. "He ran away, Grace, into the mountains. We had a place to stay last night—did some chores for board—but I . . . I can't afford a horse. I wouldn't ask, except that he may be in serious danger—"

"Sit down," said Grace, surprising him.

"Gio might be—"

"*Sit down,*" she repeated, leading him by the hands to the kitchen table. "I'll tell Sam to saddle horses, but that will take a few minutes. You'll go farther if you have a good breakfast."

"How am I supposed to—"

"*Eat,*" repeated Grace, throwing one of the servants' shawl over her shoulders, and vanished out the back door.

Reluctant but unwilling to disobey, Jon helped himself to a muffin. Only as he swallowed it did he remember that he hadn't eaten anything since the previous night's spare supper.

How hungry was Gio right now?

Not three minutes later, Grace was back, shaking off the chill spring morning.

"Now, tell me what happened," she said, immediately starting to pack a basket with bits of food from the larder. She wrapped a loaf of bread in a checked napkin and cut a hunk of cheese. *Supplies,* he realized, finishing his muffin. "Sam will fetch me as soon as the horses are ready."

"I was pretty angry with Gio last night," he admitted.

"The silver?"

He nodded. Gio had told him flat out that he wasn't the one stealing the Sullivans' silver; then it appeared in one of the boy's favorite hiding places?

You said if I told you I'd done it, you would beat me, Gio had reminded him. As if that made it all right that he'd stolen from the family that was feeding them—from Grace's family! As if that made up for Jon's abrupt expulsion from the Sullivan house . . .

Jon knew full well that he would have been thrown out anyway, having been caught kissing Grace. But he'd let the kid believe it was all over the silver. And now . . .

"I'm not responsible enough to take care of a little boy."

"Of course you are."

"Except that I didn't! I woke up this morning,

and he was long gone. All I found was this." And he handed her the awkwardly scrawled note Gio had managed to leave for him, a note he'd already memorized.

I will find our own silver, Gio had written. *I know where to look. Then Miss Grace will not be angry.*

His throat squeezed shut, just watching Grace reread those foolish, childish words. He'd been an idiot to take Gio with him, no matter how badly the Sullivans had behaved. He should have left the kid in an orphanage, where he would be safe. Now . . .

"There's still snow in the hills," Jon said. "And I don't have the slightest idea where to start looking for him."

To his relief, Grace whispered, "I think I do."

Then he saw the fear in her eyes.

Chapter Seventeen

The cold spring air made Grace's face tingle above her protective scarf and her eyes burn. If she weren't so worried about Gio, she would have loved it. She usually enjoyed the scent of the horses against the mountain air. She enjoyed riding again, even sidesaddle. She could love being alone with Jon, tiny against the expanse of the Rocky Mountains.

But the breeze smelled like snow. If they didn't find Gio before nightfall, the Rockies would turn deadly.

Of course Jon had protested Grace coming along, but she refused to stay behind. Perhaps if she knew where Da had gone, now that her mother had sent him away, she could have requested his help. Her father might be furious at Jon, but even Da's Irish temper wouldn't keep him from helping a child in danger—especially not at one of his own claims.

But with Da gone and Mama so angry, it was up to Grace. Even Belle's and Charisma's future husbands would be of little help here. So she'd left word with Phronsy, and she and Jon had ridden out together.

"Just a few more miles," she called to Jon, eyeing the puddles of new snow still unmelted in the shadow of evergreens.

It had been a long time since she'd visited the site of her father's first big strike, but heaven knew the family talked about it enough. In fact, she clearly remembered Da mentioning the Grace of God mine and how he thought it still had some silver left, while she and Gio had been hidden in the armoire. She remembered how the boy had caught his breath at the information. At the time, she'd thought he was worried about getting caught, but now . . .

It was the closest thing to a sure bet, she imagined, that a child his age could have gotten.

By the time she and Jon rode to the mine's boarded-up, snow-drifted entrance, Grace's nose had gone numb. When she saw the tunnel dug into a low drift, under and past the makeshift blockade, she feared her heart would go numb, too.

It was a Gio-sized hole, and it had been dug since the previous night's snowfall.

"Damn it." Jon swung from his saddle, wincing as he landed, either from his almost-healed leg or his sore wrist. He'd had a difficult time riding with his leg still in a cast—almost as hard a time, she thought, as he'd had asking to borrow a horse. But he hadn't complained about either.

He'd done what needed doing. She loved that about him.

"*Damn it,*" he repeated, then looked apologetically over his shoulder. "Sorry."

"I *have* heard worse." Grace dismounted before he could limp over to help her, and together they examined the snow tunnel. "You know how my parents . . ."

But she hadn't admitted to Jon yet that her father had moved out. She didn't mean to, either—not with Gio to worry about. Instead, she swallowed back pain at the sharp reminder of her family's disintegration and stayed quiet.

"Gio!" shouted Jon.

Nothing.

He began to dig with mittened hands. Grace sank to her knees in the grainy snow to help, but Jon dug much more quickly.

"If he's alive," he muttered, "I may just kill him."

Grace just kept digging. Her hands felt stiff and artificial by the time they'd reached the hole between the boards. Jon made her stand back as he broke a larger way in, snapping old boards with his bare strength. He crawled through first, unsure what they would find beyond the entrance.

While he did, Grace got a lantern and her basket of emergency rations from the horses. By the time Jon peeked back out, his handsome face drawn, she was waiting for him.

"Take these."

"You're staying out there," he protested, nevertheless accepting the bundles she handed him.

"But it's warmer inside," she said, and narrowing his eyes, Jon obediently backed up so that Grace, too, could crawl into the cold, dank mouth of the Grace of God mine.

So here was the place that had changed her family's lives forever. It felt strangely still, expectant. And it was so dark, despite streaks of wintery sunlight creeping between the boards, that she couldn't even see Jon's face until he lit the lantern.

"He must be so scared," she whispered.

Jon said, "He should be. These places are dangerous. Take my arm."

Gladly Grace did. She carried the basket, and Jon carried the light. Together they made their way tentatively around the first corner of what would surely be a labyrinth of tunnels.

"I've never seen anything so dark," Grace whispered.

Jon said, "Yeah."

"You really want to work in something like this?"

"No," he said.

Grace didn't realize how much she'd wanted to hear him say that, until she turned to look at him— and read the disappointment in his expression in the pool of lantern light.

"I don't want to dig underground," he clarified. "Not for silver."

"Oh."

"I'm here to pan for gold. Like the forty-niners."

She nodded, wishing he'd stop talking. With Gio in danger, she felt guilty to begrudge Jon his dreams of striking it rich.

It was not as if he'd ever offered her anything that his pursuit of gold would rescind.

"Gio!" she called. Her voice echoed back at her as if something inhuman, deep from the guts of the black earth, were mocking her.

Jon loosened the scarf around his neck with his free hand. Grace followed his lead. Without wind or snow, the still air of the mine was warmer than outside.

"Gio!" he called.

The Grace of God threw his voice back at them.

"Careful," he warned suddenly, catching her elbow with his free hand.

Grace sidestepped a beam that straddled the tunnel they were descending, more glad not to have tripped than she'd been in some time. "Maybe I'm wrong," she suggested, fully aware from her father's stories of the dangers that awaited a little boy down here. "Maybe he went somewhere else."

Then the tiny pool of light from the lantern caught a bundle of cloth, and he limped hurriedly closer. It was a small coat and scarf, both of which Grace had given Gio since her discovery of the boy in Jon's room.

"Gio!" they shouted in unison.

Then, from deeper down the throat of the mine, they heard a muffled cry in response.

Jon limped ahead so quickly that Grace had to drop his arm to keep her balance. She ran after him, chasing the skittering light from his swinging lantern, then skidded to a stop when he abruptly halted in front of her.

"*Uff da,*" he breathed.

Somehow, *somehow* Grace managed not to run into Jon. When she peeked around him to see why he'd stopped, she found herself looking into a pit so deep that the light from the lantern couldn't find the bottom.

"Oh, my," she whispered.

Her voice echoed down the pit, as if bouncing off walls as it fell, fell, fell. *Oh, my . . . Oh, my . . .*

"Gio!" she cried, afraid the boy had fallen and was somewhere far, far below. *Gio . . . Gio . . .*

When she heard a return call—*"Miss Grace?"*—she grasped Jon's arm to keep from falling in sheer relief. The voice came from ahead of them, farther down the tunnel, not below.

They just had to get past *below* in order to get *down the tunnel.*

"It's me, Gio," she assured him.

The boy's voice was shrill with distress. "Where is Jon?"

"I'm right here, kid," called Jon. For Grace, he pointed toward the edge of the shaft. A single beam of wood, like the ones used to shore up the mine's walls, spanned the depthless pit. "We're here to get you."

Grace looked from the narrow beam to Jon's eyes, pale in the flickering lamplight. Had Gio crossed that?

"I am scared," called the boy, his thready voice wavering. "The rock got crumbly, and I am stuck."

Crumbly? By the way Jon glanced nervously at Grace, he understood the danger of that as well as anybody. "Is it *still* crumbly, Gio?"

"Yes."

So much for any ideas Grace might have about going back to town for help.

"I'm coming," called Jon firmly. Then he said to Grace, "You're staying here."

She looked at the single beam, over a drop of who-knew-what depths, and did not mind Jon telling her what to do. She was scared, too, like Gio.

"There could be a danger of cave-ins," insisted Jon, as if she'd argued.

"All right," she said.

"I mean it," he said. But he didn't move.

Grace raised her voice and called, "Jon's coming for you, Gio." Her words echoed from below them. *Gio . . . Gio . . . Gio . . .*

Gio's voice drifted back to them. "Is he angry?"

"Yes," called Jon.

Gio said nothing.

Jon added, "But I'm coming for you anyway."

But he didn't move.

"What's wrong?" she whispered.

"I don't think . . ." But he shook his head. "Never mind." And he stepped onto the beam with his good foot.

The light reflecting off the tunnel walls began to sway. He carefully drew his other leg, in its plaster cast, ahead of him, and the light's dance became erratic. He said, "Oh, God."

Grace reached forward and grasped his hand, holding tight as he swung his bad leg back to safe ground and then—with an awkward hop—followed it with the rest of him. "Damn," he muttered. "*Damn* it! I can't do it."

That last came out almost wonderingly. As if Jon had always believed he could do anything.

Grace didn't blame him—for the confidence, which she loved, or the bad balance. "That thing on your leg has to be very heavy."

Jon took a deep breath, then said, "Too damn bad."

And he stepped awkwardly forward, almost missing the beam altogether.

"No!" Grace grabbed his arm and held it with both hands. If he had trouble crossing the beam weighed down by the plaster-of-paris cast on his leg, he should have a doubly hard time weighed down by *her.* "I'll go."

"Don't be ridiculous."

"I'm not being ridiculous; I'm being practical. If you fall off that beam, you won't be of any help to Gio, and I couldn't stand it."

Jon searched her eyes in the flickering lamplight. "You couldn't stand me not being of any help to Gio?"

The words came out teasing, but she heard an undercurrent of concern beneath them. He wanted to know what she hadn't answered the day before. He wanted to know how she felt about him.

"I couldn't stand you falling off that beam," she clarified softly, then drew her shoulders back. "I won't be clumsy this time, I promise. Normally, I don't hurt myself anyway, just other people, and as long as you stand back, you should—"

She stopped talking because Jon kissed her.

Oh, she hoped he would kiss her again when she got back with Gio. She really, truly hoped she would not fall off the beam.

"Only if you let me tie you," he said as he straightened slowly, reluctantly, from their kiss.

For a long, kiss-blurred, blue-eyes-confused moment, Grace wasn't sure what he'd said. Then she wasn't sure what he'd meant. Then she understood, and she loved him for it.

"You really think I can do it?"

Jon frowned, and his voice cracked as he asked, "Don't *you* think you can do it?"

Grace considered all the many times she'd fallen. Tripped. Hit things. Broken things. Last summer, she'd wanted to leave her clumsiness behind so badly that she'd wished for it at a rock formation in the Garden of the Gods. It had seemed like the only way.

But it wasn't.

"Yes," she told him. "I can do it. All I have to do is listen to my heart."

He grinned then, as if he understood her completely. Maybe he did.

Then he said, "But I'm still tying you. Just in case."

"I should hope so," said Grace.

Jon hated this. He truly, wholly hated this. More than he'd hated spending over a month trapped in the small, overheated room in the Sullivan mansion when he'd really wanted to be out in the mountains.

He did not want to be the one hanging back while Grace—*his* Grace—risked her life to get Gio.

But it had nothing to do with his lack of confidence in her. Not in her specifically. That beam would be difficult for anybody, not just a young lady with an awkward past.

Still, he didn't exactly have a choice. So he left poor Grace in the darkness as he hurried, limping, back to the cold day and the horses, and he got the coil of rope he'd brought. When he hobbled back into the tunnel, echoing bits of Grace's singing bounced toward him from its depths:

"Out on the prairie one bright, starry night,
They broke out the whiskey, and Betsy got tight.
She sang and she shouted and she danced o'er the

*plain, And she showed her bare arse to the whole
wagon train. . . ."*

As he got closer, Jon could hear that Gio was
even singing along with the chorus: *"Singing too-ra-
li-oo-ra-li-oo-ra-li-ay."*

The thought of the two of them singing salty
mining-camp songs to each other for companionship in the deepest dark, struck him so deeply it
hurt. Somehow, he had to find a way to get them
out safe.

Both of them.

If he couldn't trust his own leg or his own balance, he could do a lot worse than trust Grace.

"Here," he said, tying the rope tightly around her
waist. "I'm going to hang on to this end and only let
out a little bit at a time. That way if you fall—"

"I won't," she said with surprising confidence.

He kissed her again. He couldn't help it. "I know
you won't," he said, as if he hadn't. As if he didn't
love her so deeply, his chest might implode. "But it
gives me something to do. If the ground gives way
beneath you, or you get lost, this rope may help. All
right?"

"All right." Grace stepped to the edge of the
shaft, hesitated, then looked back at him. *"Jon?"*

It was there in her beautiful, true-blue eyes. *I love
you.*

He'd never wanted to hear those words so badly
in all his life. But not yet. Not if she . . .

"Tell me when you get back," he said.

She nodded, picked up the lamp, and stepped
out onto the too-narrow beam.

Jon opened his mouth to beg her not to carry
the basket with her, but by then she'd already taken

two more steps. He tightened his hold on the rope, too aware that it did not ensure her safety if she fell. Better to let her continue as she wished than to confuse matters now.

Another step. Another.

To his relief, Grace scooted effortlessly across the old beam, lunch basket and all.

"She made it!" Jon called to Gio, as soon as she reached the other side.

"Hurry!" Gio's voice from the darkness shook. "The wall is crumbling more."

Oh, God.

"I'm coming," promised Grace, and glanced back toward Jon one last time. Lamplight lit the satisfaction in her beautiful face. "I'll bring you back safe and sound."

Then she hurried on, her light shrinking into the blackness, Jon feeding out the rope he'd tied to her as he might an ice-fishing line. He kept a length of it wrapped around one or the other of his hands at all times. He wasn't about to lose Grace to some damned mine. Not now. Not ever.

Even if that meant jilting Fortune and Destiny like yesterday's news.

In only a moment, Jon was alone in the purest darkness that existed—the darkness of underground. The only connection he had to Grace was the rope, and the sound of her echoing voice:

> *"They stopped at Salt Lake to inquire of the way,*
> *When Brigham declared that Sweet Betsy should stay.*
>
> *Poor Betsy got frightened and ran like—"*

Unable to see a thing, Jon only heard it at first. Heard it in the silence of Grace's faltering voice. The faintest patter of rocks and pebbles hitting the stone floor at his feet. No . . .

Then harder impacts. Something struck his shoulder like a hailstone.

God, no.

Then the rumble.

"Gio!" Jon called, trying to haul the rope back. *"GRACE!"*

Then, with an earthy roar, the world collapsed in on him.

Chapter Eighteen

When he first opened his eyes after the cave-in, Jon thought he might be dead. Then he inhaled a mouthful of dust and choked so violently, he knew he must still be among the living.

Somewhere in a vast, underground darkness.

"Grace?" The name stuttered from his throat, with his first true breath, and he gasped air for another. "Gio? *Grace!*"

He pushed himself upward—what seemed like upward—and felt rocks and rubble skid off his back, heard them thud to the invisible floor beneath him. He tightened his right hand—and realized it held nothing.

No!

His left—also empty.

He'd lost the rope. His only connection to her, and he'd lost it.

"Grace!" he screamed, and crawled blindly forward. Rocks cut at his palms; he wrenched his weak wrist. Still he patted the ground, edging in the direction he'd gone . . .

Until his hand found nothingness. The edge of the shaft.

Jon knew from experience that those mine shafts

could go down hundreds, even thousands, of feet. He hadn't been able to cross the beam even by lantern light, even before he'd been swallowed up by the cave-in. Now he fumbled for it anyway, determined not to leave the two people he most . . .

. . . most *loved* . . .

. . . alone in this impromptu grave.

The beam wasn't there. His outstretched hands searched the entire length of the precipice again, again finding nothing. It must have fallen during the cave-in.

He couldn't reach them. Whether they lived . . . or not.

Not by himself, he couldn't.

Jon didn't know how much later he finally saw light—he couldn't tell how much time had even passed before he resolved to dig his way out of the mine, alone. Somehow, the bright afternoon light felt like failure. He hadn't kept Gio or Grace safe. How much worse a failure could that be?

But he'd had plenty of time to think while crawling blindly toward the mouth of the tunnel. He did have a plan.

Determined, he mounted his borrowed horse and rode back to Grace's town and the family she'd been so loath to leave.

Funny how he'd found it so very difficult, just this morning, to borrow one of the Sullivans' horses. It had felt like asking for charity.

In contrast, going to Patrick Sullivan and admitting that he may have just gotten his daughter killed seemed like the easiest thing in the world.

After all, it was Grace's only hope.

And if he had gotten her killed, he didn't care what happened next anyway.

Two sleepless days later, amid the chaos of a town-wide rescue effort, Jon was losing hope. He'd worked at digging until his bad wrist gave out, then tried to do it one-handed. When workers from Patrick Sullivan's larger mines pushed him brusquely out of the way, Jon joined the scores of men carrying out rocks. That, he also did one-handed and limping.

He felt dizzy with exhaustion and, worse, with guilt.

If he hadn't been so determined to have adventure . . . if he hadn't hidden Gio for so long . . . if he'd approached Patrick Sullivan as soon as he knew he had feelings for the man's youngest daughter . . . How many chances had Jon been given to improve this outcome? How many had he ignored?

He couldn't forget how Patrick Sullivan's expression had changed from suspicion to horror when Jon finally tracked the man down at his office. He still couldn't face Mrs. Sullivan or Grace's sisters. All he could do was keep working, to numb the pain of it, and to pray. To pray for Grace, in every sense of the word.

Maybe if he worked hard enough, if he was willing to sacrifice enough, God would let her and Gio be safe.

But if they didn't have air, then even if they'd survived the initial cave-in there was little hope.

Jon wasn't even sure what day it was when, as he

staggered from the mouth of the mine with more rocks, four strong hands caught him and pulled him aside.

"Rest," commanded Will Barclay, helping Kit Stanhope shove Jon down onto a large boulder amid the pine trees overlooking the rescue efforts. "You'll be of no good to Grace if you work yourself to death before they find her."

Assuming they *did* find her.

Jon wasn't sure he'd be of any good to her alive, either. But he didn't have the energy to fight back. When Stanhope pressed a mug of hot coffee into his hands, Jon took it.

He even took a sip. The cramping in his stomach made him wonder how long it had been since he'd eaten anything.

Since Grace and Gio were still trapped, it clearly hadn't been long enough.

"Thank you," he managed—only a bare hint of courtesy. Then, as Stanhope handed him a muffin, it occurred to Jon to question their presence. "You know about me and Grace?"

"Belle and Charisma told us about it," said Barclay. "The workers are trying to keep the ladies away from the mine itself—you can imagine how that is going over with Charisma!"

Stanhope took up the explanation. "So they asked us to check on you."

Despite how good the muffin smelled to Jon on his empty stomach, he couldn't bring himself to take a bite. His eyes burned suspiciously. "They should hate me."

"If Grace loves you," said Stanhope, "that's not

likely. Besides, the cook told us how you tried to talk Grace out of going with you."

"It's hard to stop a Sullivan," agreed Barclay. "Trust us. We know."

Unsure what to say to that, Jon ate the muffin and drank his coffee and watched the rescue efforts. Somehow, Patrick Sullivan had gotten some mining equipment up the mountainside; he was overseeing the workers who knew how to run it, speeding up the efforts to dig out the tunnel and shore up its walls. Townsmen from millionaires to the lowest laborers were pitching in, trying desperately to save one of their own—and a little boy who wasn't even that.

Jon recognized Robert James through a mask of mud. Stanhope and Barclay were equally filthy from their shifts in the dirt.

He could tell from the slushy mud that it had snowed again since he and Grace had first gone into the Grace of God. "What day is it?"

"Saturday." Stanhope didn't look at him. "The mayor has canceled the Founder's Day ball."

Oh. Staring down at his mug, Jon said, "Grace put a lot of stock into going to that."

"Grace," said Stanhope, "put a lot of stock into many things. I believe they may have been the wise priorities. Notice Sullivan out there."

Jon could hardly keep his eyes off the man whose daughter he'd lost. Despite the pain etched across Paddy Sullivan's face, Grace's father was in the middle of the rescue efforts. "He's good at this."

Barclay said, "I believe this may be the first time he's truly appreciated his wealth. The manpower, the machinery, the rewards he's offered—he could never have responded this quickly or this thoroughly if it weren't for his money."

"And that muffin you just ate?" Stanhope nodded far across the clearing to where several tents had been set up for the women of the town to help in their own way. "Bridget Sullivan made it."

"Charisma said she hasn't stopped baking since she heard the news," added Barclay. "Feeding the rescue workers gives her something to do, social standing be damned."

Charisma. Jon felt another pang of guilt. "How are Grace's sisters?"

Stanhope said, "As well as can be expected. They—"

But a shout from the mouth of the mine caught their attention. Jon dropped the mug as he stood, and started limping in that direction. Stanhope and Barclay followed, but word reached them before they reached the Grace of God.

". . . They found the rope . . ."

". . . The diggers found Erikson's rope. . . ."

". . . It shouldn't be long now. . . ."

Jon's limp became a hitching run as he left the other Sullivan beaux behind him to reach the mine. The main tunnel of the Grace of God was well lit now, with lanterns every ten feet or so, and Jon had no trouble seeing to hobble his way through the workers. They'd built a solid bridge across the shaft that Grace had so easily crossed several days earlier. Soon Jon found the area of rubble yet to be cleared.

Sure enough, the men were pulling rocks away from the rope that had been supposed to protect Grace—the one he'd lost when the world caved in.

Patrick Sullivan was one of those men, using his bare hands. He looked up, his expression unreadable in the flickering lamplight, as Jon arrived.

"Best get to it, boyo," he said shortly.

And Jon began digging out rocks as well, with his good hand, as fast as he could.

They uncovered more rope. Then more. Whoever had said it wouldn't be long now had been right.

But what would they find?

Then, above the muttering of men and the thud of rocks, Jon heard something. "Quiet!"

The men around him fell silent—even Grace's father. Several frowned when they heard nothing.

Then the sound repeated—a whistle.

It was a song most of the rescue workers, being miners, recognized: "The Days of Forty-Nine." One of Grace's favorite camp songs.

If Jon could have fallen to his knees in gratitude, he would have. The cast kept him from it, so he showed his gratitude by digging faster. Grace was alive. She was alive! Even if she never wanted to see him, he could breathe again, could live again, because she lived.

If she'd reached Gio, the boy should be okay, too.

He had no doubts of Grace's ability to do that.

He had no doubts about Grace at all.

Grace had found Gio, his eyes large with fear and pain and his foot pinned under a rock, just before the walls tumbled in. When that happened, she dropped both the basket and the lantern to cover him with her own body.

Cave-ins, she learned, *hurt*. Rocks hit her back and shoulders and even her head, so that her ears rang. But the Grace of God mine lived up to its name. She could think of no reason besides the grace of God that the section of tunnel arched over her and Gio did not completely collapse.

Once the noise subsided and she and Gio sat up blindly, coughing and holding each other, the Grace of God came through again. By fumbling around in the suffocating darkness, Grace couldn't find the lantern Jon had sent with her.

But she found her basket of food.

"Where's Jon?" asked Gio, his voice aching with both the need to trust in his hero and the terror that his trust would prove misplaced.

"He's going back for help," said Grace—past an almost unbearable ache in her own chest. She might be lying. Jon might be buried under tons of Rocky Mountain even now. She and Gio might merely be facing a slower death.

But she remembered what Phronsy had said, and she listened to her heart, and her heart told her to hope.

So they sat together and waited.

And waited.

And ate some bread and cheese, and waited.

Gio told her about his parents and his life in the Bowery of New York City before his papa took him west. Grace told him about her childhood in Leadville, and how simple everything had seemed.

"This is why you must marry Jon and become my

mother," said Gio, with total confidence. "To make things simple again."

Grace could think of little that was less simple than her and Jon . . . except that, again, her heart disagreed.

The idea that she may never again breathe fresh air or see her family or even the sun again made some aspects of life seem clear. One of those was that no matter how complicated things became, she must not lose Jon.

Assuming you have not already, whispered a frightened corner of her mind. It was so very dark, like drowning. And she could feel the waiting heaviness of the rocks all around them. And Jon had been so very close to that mine shaft. . . .

That was when she began to teach Gio more camp songs. As easily as Grace might have panicked, Gio gave her reason not to. For the boy, she would remain cheerful and confident. Even if they died down here, Gio need not die any more frightened than he already was.

An eternity seemed to pass. Gio fell asleep, and Grace decided to join him, unsure if she would ever wake. If they were losing air down here . . .

But she did wake, to continued blackness and to the continued need to put on a good face—even if the little boy could not see it.

And somehow, by convincing Gio that they would escape this safely, Grace practically convinced herself.

Practically.

They ran out of word games to play. They emptied the basket and grew very, very thirsty. As exhaustion set in—the kind of exhaustion that no amount of naps would counter—Grace turned to her earliest memories of comfort, of her family's lost closeness, and of the camp songs.

"Oh, I miss the boys and all the noise, and the gold that once was mine," she sang. And when she had no more voice, she whistled. She knew that Comtesse Arabella would disapprove as surely as would her mother, who'd always said that "Whistling girls and crowing hens always come to bad ends."

An ironic prediction, considering . . .

But Grace had no intention of letting anyone else's likes and dislikes dictate her own life ever again. So she held Gio, and she taught him to whistle, too. . . .

And when rocks to the side of them crumbled away, letting in the first light they'd seen in what had to be days, Grace squinted up at her reward:

Jon Erikson's drawn, worried face. His safe, *alive* face.

"Jon!" she croaked, wishing she had more voice, and then her view of him vanished as other miners surged forward, including her father. She tried to tell them that Gio was stuck, but they saw that and they set about freeing him. She was glad to see her father, so very glad to be pulled tight into Da's filthy, sweaty embrace, like when she was a child. But still, she had to find . . .

There. Dragging himself, cast and all, through the passage the others had made, there was Jon, come to get her.

Grace hurled herself at him, not the least bit worried that she would hurt him, and he caught her with ease. "Oh, Gracie," whispered Jon, squeezing her so hard it hurt—but it hurt wonderfully. He kissed her head, her face, her ears, while she kissed his, and he gasped her name after each kiss. "Oh, Grace."

"I didn't do it," she said, hoarse. "I didn't make the mountain fall down."

Jon laughed. "Oh, darling, I never thought you did."

Darling?

That stunned her long enough for Jon to reach past her and swing little Gio up into his embrace, so that the boy was squooshed between the two of them.

"Are you angry at me?" asked Gio.

"Yes," said Jon, and kissed him on the head. "I'm angry at you, and I want you to stay with Grace and me, wherever we decide to live. If she'll have—"

Grace kissed him, to silence all doubts he might try to express. "Don't you dare doubt that I'll have you, Jon Erikson! I'd have you if you were a dirt *farmer,* let alone a miner."

"I don't have to prospect," Jon assured her, smiling down at her as if she were everything important to him. "*You're* my fortune, Grace. *You're* my destiny."

She'd never felt so loved. "Of course you'll prospect. And I'll bake, to earn extra money. We'll find a place close enough that my family can visit, but far enough that they won't drive you crazy."

Someone cleared his throat beside them. That was when Grace finally noticed all the miners watching them, most of them grinning through dark masks of sweat-hardened grit. She noticed them and her father standing right next to them.

"And am I not getting a say in any of this?" asked Da.

"No, Da," said Grace lovingly. "You don't."

To her surprise, Da joined the other miners with his grin. "As it should be, Gracie girl. As it should be. But Bridey will be having my head if I don't bring you to her and your sisters right away. Mine and young Erikson's, both."

To Grace's delight, both men slid an arm over her shoulder from either side, to lead her out. Jon carried Gio on one hip, despite his own limp.

"Da? Does this mean you and Mama are talking again? That you aren't moving out?"

"No promises," Da warned her. "But these last few days have put some matters into perspective for us both."

Grace thought she could not feel happier, until Jon leaned close to her ear and whispered, "I almost forgot. I love you. Please marry me."

She whispered back, "You didn't think I would move off to mine with you otherwise, do you?"

She had no idea how to read his grin, except to see the love in it.

"I love you, too," she said, and his grin widened, and his arm on her shoulders tightened.

To her surprise, Da stepped forward to lead the way, letting her go. She felt a sweet pang at the rightness of it.

Gio, unaware of the dynamics being completed, said, "Phronsy, the cook, told me of a place in the mountains where we can prospect."

"Did she?" asked Jon, gazing at Grace.

"Yes," said the boy. "It would be perfect for you, Jon. It is called Cripple Creek."

"Very funny," said Jon, still gazing at Grace.

"I think it sounds wonderful," she said.

But with the three of them emerging into the spring air and the sunshine, and her mother and sisters rushing forward to embrace her, and Jon at her side, everything in the world seemed wonderful.

Thank you, she thought heavenward—yet another important meaning of the word *grace.*

She thought she caught sight of their cook, Phronsy, at the edge of the crowd, before she and Jon were circled by loving family and friends.

Phronsy was smiling.

So was Grace.

Epilogue

That autumn saw the wedding of the year as the three Sullivan sisters married their true loves—in the beautiful rocky Garden of the Gods. The mild mountain breeze and the gentle sunshine all seemed specially ordered for the occasion.

All of Colorado Springs turned out, as did much of Colorado's political elite, several landed families from England, and a surprising number of the miners from silver king Patrick Sullivan's mines.

Everyone agreed that though all three girls were very pretty, nobody had seen a more beautiful bride than Belle Sullivan. Charisma, who had once seemed so blunt and improper, was the epitome of charm. And Grace seemed to have outgrown the childish clumsiness which had haunted her for so long.

Nobody but her family knew that was because she tended to be more surefooted out of doors . . . and when she knew Jon was around.

During the ceremony, all three brides sneaked happy glances at their parents, who had in the past half year rediscovered their own romance and were even now holding hands. But for the most part, Belle only had eyes for Christopher Stanhope.

Charisma cared for little beyond William Barclay. And Grace managed to lose herself yet again in the summertime blue gaze of her Norwegian miner, Jon Erikson.

It was safe to do that, now—just as it would be safe, tonight, finally to learn what Belle and Charisma had discovered by crossing those invisible lines of propriety.

Will Barclay had already helped Jon adopt Gio, who had Americanized his name as Joe Erikson. "Joe" would be staying with his new grandparents during the honeymoon.

Once Bridey Sullivan accepted that all three daughters were safe and happy, and that she need not pursue social acceptance quite so passionately, she'd come to see what a charming little boy Joe could be.

Not long after, she'd sent Comtesse Arabella packing.

Joe sat between Bridey and Patrick, swinging his high-booted feet and keeping an eye on everything, occasionally scratching where his adorable Little Lord Fauntleroy outfit itched.

"By the powers vested in me," pronounced the minister, "I now pronounce you men and wives. You may kiss—"

But the three couples were already kissing.

Patrick Sullivan had spared no expense setting up a bountiful reception amid the soaring rock formations of the Garden of the Gods, and he stood to invite their guests to join them. Belle, Charisma, and Grace took advantage of the milling crowd to draw their new husbands off behind some rocks.

"No, not for that," laughed Belle Stanhope as Kit

willingly kissed down her milky neck. "We have to show you something."

"Really?" asked Will, raising his eyebrows with interest. Charisma Barclay elbowed him in the side, with a grin.

Jon tightened his hold around Grace Erikson's slim waist, telling her with his gaze that he was as excited about their wedding night as she was. But all he said was, "You know I'd follow you anywhere, Gracie."

"It's not far," she insisted, drawing him with her as the sisters headed toward three elegant finger-like spires of tiered heights that reached toward the sky. "This is called the Three Graces. We were named after them."

Belle tightened her grip on Kit's hand—of their three new husbands, he was the only one who'd been there from the start. "It's where our father proposed to our mother."

Charisma's eyes danced as she confessed to her husband and the others, "And one more thing— but that's our secret."

Will said, "It looks as if someone else might be enjoying the park today, ladies."

Indeed, three women stood at the base of the monument, wearing what looked like . . . togas?

Kit slowed his step. "Isn't that your dressmaker, Belle? Madama Aglaia?"

Charisma caught her breath. "And the widow Poppadopoulos, the senator's wife. Whatever is she doing here?"

Grace bounced with recognition and, despite the simple elegance of her full-skirted white gown, waved. "And it's our cook, Phronsy. Hello, Phronsy! Where did you go?"

The three women waved back.

"What an odd assortment of women," mused Will.

Kit said, "What an ironic assortment, you mean."

The others looked at him, confused.

"Belle's dressmaker, and our matchmaker, was Madame Aglaia," explained Kit. "And Jon told me how helpful Phronsy—short for Euphrosyne, yes?—was during his courtship of Grace."

Jon said, "You're getting at something, Stanhope."

The blond Englishman said, "I merely wonder if the widow Poppadopoulos has the Christian name of Thalia."

Slowly Will said, "I believe you're right!"

Their wives stared at them, still not understanding. Neither did Jon, who said, "And that's ironic because . . . ?"

"Because the Three Graces of Greek mythology were named Aglaia, Thalia, and Euphrosyne," explained Kit. "Aglaia was the archetype of beauty, Thalia was the archetype of charm, and Eurphrosyne—"

"Represented grace," finished Charisma.

The six of them looked back toward the monument—and the three women were gone.

"You don't think . . . !" whispered Grace.

"Likely, they've gone to the reception," said Will. "Shall we do the same?"

But as they headed in that direction, Belle drew her two sisters back. "*Do* you think it could have been them?"

"If it was," whispered Charisma, "they certainly granted our wishes."

"They did better than that." Grace glanced once more over her shoulder at the rock formation and mouthed, *Thank you*. Then she hurried forward and caught Jon's hand.

He drew her tightly to his side, where they both belonged.

The Three Graces may well have tutored the Sullivan girls in beauty, charm, and grace.

But what was more, the Sullivans had found love.

Discover the Thrill of Romance with
Lisa Plumley

__Making Over Mike
0-8217-7110-8 $5.99US/$7.99CAN

Amanda Connor is a life coach—not a magician! Granted, as a publicity stunt for her new business, the savvy entrepreneur has promised to transform some poor slob into a perfectly balanced example of modern manhood. But Mike Cavaco gives "raw material" new meaning.

__Falling for April
0-8217-7111-6 $5.99US/$7.99CAN

Her hometown gourmet catering company may be in a slump, but April Finnegan isn't about to begin again. Determined to save her business, she sets out to win some local sponsors, unaware she's not the only one with that idea. Turns out wealthy department store mogul Ryan Forrester is one step—and thousands of dollars—ahead of her.

__Reconsidering Riley
0-8217-7340-2 $5.99US/$7.99CAN

Jayne Murphy's best-selling relationship manual *Heartbreak 101* was inspired by her all-too-personal experience with gorgeous, capable . . . *outdoorsy* . . . Riley Davis, who stole her heart—and promptly skipped town with it. Now, Jayne's organized a workshop for dumpees. But it becomes hell on her heart when the leader for her group's week-long nature jaunt turns out to be none other than a certain . . .

Available Wherever Books Are Sold!

Visit our website at **www.kensingtonbooks.com**.